NO FEAR

(A Valerie Law FBI Suspense Thriller —Book Three)

BLAKE PIERCE

Blake Pierce

Blake Pierce is the USA Today bestselling author of the RILEY PAGE mystery series, which includes seventeen books. Blake Pierce is also the author of the MACKENZIE WHITE mystery series, comprising fourteen books; of the AVERY BLACK mystery series, comprising six books; of the KERI LOCKE mystery series, comprising five books; of the MAKING OF RILEY PAIGE mystery series, comprising six books; of the KATE WISE mystery series, comprising seven books; of the CHLOE FINE psychological suspense mystery, comprising six books; of the JESSE HUNT psychological suspense thriller series, comprising twenty four books; of the AU PAIR psychological suspense thriller series, comprising three books; of the ZOE PRIME mystery series, comprising six books; of the ADELE SHARP mystery series, comprising fifteen books, of the EUROPEAN VOYAGE cozy mystery series, comprising four books; of the new LAURA FROST FBI suspense thriller, comprising nine books (and counting); of the new ELLA DARK FBI suspense thriller, comprising eleven books (and counting); of the A YEAR IN EUROPE cozy mystery series, comprising nine books, of the AVA GOLD mystery series, comprising six books (and counting); of the RACHEL GIFT mystery series, comprising eight books (and counting); of the VALERIE LAW mystery series, comprising nine books (and counting); of the PAIGE KING mystery series, comprising six books (and counting); of the MAY MOORE mystery series, comprising six books (and counting); and the CORA SHIELDS mystery series, comprising three books (and counting).

An avid reader and lifelong fan of the mystery and thriller genres, Blake loves to hear from you, so please feel free to visit www.blakepierceauthor.com to learn more and stay in touch.

HER LAST CHANCE (Book #2)
HER LAST HOPE (Book #3)
HER LAST FEAR (Book #4)
HER LAST CHOICE (Book #5)
HER LAST BREATH (Book #6)
HER LAST MISTAKE (Book #7)
HER LAST DESIRE (Book #8)

AVA GOLD MYSTERY SERIES
CITY OF PREY (Book #1)
CITY OF FEAR (Book #2)
CITY OF BONES (Book #3)
CITY OF GHOSTS (Book #4)
CITY OF DEATH (Book #5)
CITY OF VICE (Book #6)

A YEAR IN EUROPE
A MURDER IN PARIS (Book #1)
DEATH IN FLORENCE (Book #2)
VENGEANCE IN VIENNA (Book #3)
A FATALITY IN SPAIN (Book #4)

ELLA DARK FBI SUSPENSE THRILLER
GIRL, ALONE (Book #1)
GIRL, TAKEN (Book #2)
GIRL, HUNTED (Book #3)
GIRL, SILENCED (Book #4)
GIRL, VANISHED (Book 5)
GIRL ERASED (Book #6)
GIRL, FORSAKEN (Book #7)
GIRL, TRAPPED (Book #8)
GIRL, EXPENDABLE (Book #9)
GIRL, ESCAPED (Book #10)
GIRL, HIS (Book #11)

LAURA FROST FBI SUSPENSE THRILLER
ALREADY GONE (Book #1)
ALREADY SEEN (Book #2)
ALREADY TRAPPED (Book #3)

ALREADY MISSING (Book #4)
ALREADY DEAD (Book #5)
ALREADY TAKEN (Book #6)
ALREADY CHOSEN (Book #7)
ALREADY LOST (Book #8)
ALREADY HIS (Book #9)

EUROPEAN VOYAGE COZY MYSTERY SERIES
MURDER (AND BAKLAVA) (Book #1)
DEATH (AND APPLE STRUDEL) (Book #2)
CRIME (AND LAGER) (Book #3)
MISFORTUNE (AND GOUDA) (Book #4)
CALAMITY (AND A DANISH) (Book #5)
MAYHEM (AND HERRING) (Book #6)

ADELE SHARP MYSTERY SERIES
LEFT TO DIE (Book #1)
LEFT TO RUN (Book #2)
LEFT TO HIDE (Book #3)
LEFT TO KILL (Book #4)
LEFT TO MURDER (Book #5)
LEFT TO ENVY (Book #6)
LEFT TO LAPSE (Book #7)
LEFT TO VANISH (Book #8)
LEFT TO HUNT (Book #9)
LEFT TO FEAR (Book #10)
LEFT TO PREY (Book #11)
LEFT TO LURE (Book #12)
LEFT TO CRAVE (Book #13)
LEFT TO LOATHE (Book #14)
LEFT TO HARM (Book #15)

THE AU PAIR SERIES
ALMOST GONE (Book#1)
ALMOST LOST (Book #2)
ALMOST DEAD (Book #3)

ZOE PRIME MYSTERY SERIES
FACE OF DEATH (Book#1)

FACE OF MURDER (Book #2)
FACE OF FEAR (Book #3)
FACE OF MADNESS (Book #4)
FACE OF FURY (Book #5)
FACE OF DARKNESS (Book #6)

A JESSIE HUNT PSYCHOLOGICAL SUSPENSE SERIES
THE PERFECT WIFE (Book #1)
THE PERFECT BLOCK (Book #2)
THE PERFECT HOUSE (Book #3)
THE PERFECT SMILE (Book #4)
THE PERFECT LIE (Book #5)
THE PERFECT LOOK (Book #6)
THE PERFECT AFFAIR (Book #7)
THE PERFECT ALIBI (Book #8)
THE PERFECT NEIGHBOR (Book #9)
THE PERFECT DISGUISE (Book #10)
THE PERFECT SECRET (Book #11)
THE PERFECT FAÇADE (Book #12)
THE PERFECT IMPRESSION (Book #13)
THE PERFECT DECEIT (Book #14)
THE PERFECT MISTRESS (Book #15)
THE PERFECT IMAGE (Book #16)
THE PERFECT VEIL (Book #17)
THE PERFECT INDISCRETION (Book #18)
THE PERFECT RUMOR (Book #19)
THE PERFECT COUPLE (Book #20)
THE PERFECT MURDER (Book #21)
THE PERFECT HUSBAND (Book #22)
THE PERFECT SCANDAL (Book #23)
THE PERFECT MASK (Book #24)

CHLOE FINE PSYCHOLOGICAL SUSPENSE SERIES
NEXT DOOR (Book #1)
A NEIGHBOR'S LIE (Book #2)
CUL DE SAC (Book #3)
SILENT NEIGHBOR (Book #4)
HOMECOMING (Book #5)

TINTED WINDOWS (Book #6)

KATE WISE MYSTERY SERIES
IF SHE KNEW (Book #1)
IF SHE SAW (Book #2)
IF SHE RAN (Book #3)
IF SHE HID (Book #4)
IF SHE FLED (Book #5)
IF SHE FEARED (Book #6)
IF SHE HEARD (Book #7)

THE MAKING OF RILEY PAIGE SERIES
WATCHING (Book #1)
WAITING (Book #2)
LURING (Book #3)
TAKING (Book #4)
STALKING (Book #5)
KILLING (Book #6)

RILEY PAIGE MYSTERY SERIES
ONCE GONE (Book #1)
ONCE TAKEN (Book #2)
ONCE CRAVED (Book #3)
ONCE LURED (Book #4)
ONCE HUNTED (Book #5)
ONCE PINED (Book #6)
ONCE FORSAKEN (Book #7)
ONCE COLD (Book #8)
ONCE STALKED (Book #9)
ONCE LOST (Book #10)
ONCE BURIED (Book #11)
ONCE BOUND (Book #12)
ONCE TRAPPED (Book #13)
ONCE DORMANT (Book #14)
ONCE SHUNNED (Book #15)
ONCE MISSED (Book #16)
ONCE CHOSEN (Book #17)

MACKENZIE WHITE MYSTERY SERIES

PROLOGUE

Maria held the old man's hand as the last light of life flickered in his eyes. He gasped, his eyes searching as if for a way out. But there was no way out. The old man had been in the hospital bed for two months.

A long exhale, and then he was gone.

Maria sat looking at him.

She felt so sorry for him. No family. No friends. She felt it only right that she should be there with him as he died. At least he wasn't alone; that gave her some comfort.

She stood up, straightened her white nurse's uniform, and then wiped the tears away that were welling up in her eyes.

She had been a nurse for five years. Still at a tender age. Still learning. But it had never gotten easier.

Leaning over, she touched the old man's eyelids and brought them to a close.

"Be at peace," she said quietly to him. And then she left the room to the stillness of death.

*

The hospital grounds were bathed in darkness as Maria breathed in the night air. She liked the cold nocturnal breeze, especially at the end of her shift. It reminded her she was alive. Sometimes she needed that. Being surrounded by dying patients could make you forget that life was for the living.

Maria's footsteps echoed, bouncing between the few parked cars on the south side of the main building. The lot was mostly empty by that time, hospital visitors having long since departed.

Street lights created pools of illumination, glinting off puddles that had gathered sporadically on the concrete. But there was no rain. Not now. Just the night breeze whispering over proceedings.

Maria had never liked that parking lot, especially at night. It had always felt a little too isolated, a little too dark. She had complained to

1

the hospital management about it. But they said the lighting was adequate.

It wasn't.

Her car was still some way off, and how Maria wished it had been nearer. She was beginning to feel that she was no longer alone.

As her footsteps quickened slightly, slapping occasionally against the wet surface of the parking lot, she thought she heard the slight suggestion of someone moving nearby.

She stopped and looked over her shoulder.

A few sporadic cars sat silently between her and the hospital building. No one was there, but the shadows could have been hiding anything.

Maria turned and began walking again. Finally, her parked car came into view.

But this didn't provide her with comfort. It should have, but it didn't. Instead, it only made her more anxious to reach the safety of it.

There it was again, that sound.

Another movement in the lot. And this time it was definitive: the sound of someone's clothes rustling against the smooth surface of a car.

Maria imagined a man sneaking between two parked cars, ready to pounce.

The thought sent a shiver down her spine. She looked in her handbag and felt for her car keys as she kept walking quickly.

Is someone there?

She wasn't sure if she had actually said it aloud or not. But in that moment, she didn't want to find out. There was a fear building deep inside; it fueled her apprehension. She broke into a run.

Maria could feel her heart racing in her chest as she neared the car. She was aware of the rising panic in her throat and the feeling of dread in the pit of her stomach. But she didn't want to show that someone was making her feel uneasy.

She tried to appear nonchalant and cursed herself for her anxiety. She didn't want whoever it was to sense how scared she was.

Her keys jangled in her hand as she reached her car and fumbled to open it.

She felt the door handle and pulled.

But it was locked.

"Come on! Come on!" she said, shaking the door.

The door suddenly opened, almost as if it had given up and decided to let her escape.

As she stood there for a split second, looking at the safety of her car interior, she heard that sound again. The sound of clothes rustling.

Maria turned instinctively.

Standing beside her was a man, tall, looming, and bathed in shadow. Without looking at him, she knew, she could feel it: He meant to hurt her.

As the man stepped closer, she felt the hair on her neck stand up. Her eyes were frozen open in terror, but she knew she had to move. She had to get away.

The man reached out his hand and grabbed her by the wrist with one quick motion.

"No!" she screamed. "No!"

Maria struggled to pull her arm away. She could feel the man's bony fingers digging into her skin like tiny knives.

She reached out for the safety of the car, her fingertips scraping at the open door as the man dragged her to the ground.

Maria felt the cold wetness of the parking lot as her body was slammed against it.

A pain shot up through her body.

But the pain was quickly eclipsed by terror.

The dim light caught the shape of a claw hammer, which the man brought down quickly, burying it into Maria's skull.

CHAPTER ONE

Valerie knew it had all come down to this moment, and she dreaded it.

She looked up at the exterior of Wakefield Psychiatric Institute. Its harsh gray rectangular outline cut an imposing figure against the bright sun above.

She's in there, Valerie thought. It had been many years since she had been so close to meeting her mother face-to-face. But she cared deeply for her mother's welfare, even though she didn't always want to admit it.

Her mother also had answers about Valerie's past. Particularly regarding the cryptic messages she had sent to Valerie via her sister. Valerie had tried to understand them fully, reading the crumpled pieces of paper intensely, hoping that a solution would be found.

But only her mother had the truth. And in Valerie's gut, she felt whatever that truth was, it would be earth shattering.

Valerie and her sister Suzie had grown up loving their mother, but her mental illness had left an indelible imprint on them both. Suzie was being treated for a psychiatric break down at another hospital, and Valerie, a successful FBI agent and profiler, was now terrified of her own thoughts.

How long would it be until the same illness consumed her?

She walked through the large double doors of the Wakefield Psychiatric Institute and brandished her FBI badge at the two guards watching the entrance.

They nodded and pointed Valerie to the front desk.

Valerie tried to calm her nerves as she approached. This wasn't a standard visit. For the first time in her life, she was going to use her FBI credentials to facilitate something in her personal life. She struggled with the ethical implications, but her colleague and now mentor, Doctor Will Cooper, had encouraged her to use all avenues open to her to talk with her mother. He had even encouraged her to use the FBI to track down her father, though that had so far proved a dead end.

"Hello," Valerie said to a portly woman in her sixties behind the front desk. "I'm Agent Valerie Law; I'm here to see Doctor Mellor."

"Sign here, please," the lady said, offering a clipboard. "And please leave your firearm."

Valerie pulled her revolver from its holster and handed it over. After signing, she was led through two separate security gates. Those gates kept the inmates of Wakefield from the outside world. Passing through them felt like passing into the underworld.

Finally, she was led into a small waiting room with beige walls, a plastic houseplant, and a hung painting of a schooner on an open sea. It was not exactly high art. The entire room felt to Valerie like a contrived attempt at setting visitors at ease. But the unease could not be so easily removed. It had grabbed hold of Valerie's thoughts like rot.

Valerie sat there waiting. The room was warmer than it needed to be, and she was starting to feel a little uncomfortable in her suit.

Her thoughts turned to her mother. What condition was she in?

She had been imprisoned for many years, and according to Suzie, Valerie's sister, their mother's mental health had significantly degraded over time.

That broke Valerie's heart.

For the first time in almost a decade, the worry for her mother's well-being was seeping into her everyday life. It was consuming her, even though Valerie still felt resentment towards her.

The door to the beige waiting room opened and in stepped a man in a black suit and glasses.

"Hello, Agent Law," the man said, introducing himself. "I'm Doctor Mellor, sorry for the wait."

"No problem," Valerie said, trying to remain cool and calm. That was not easy when she was about to go against her ethics. But sometimes family had to come before her professional pride. She'd put her work first for too long.

The doctor sat down on a plastic chair opposite from Valerie. He looked like he was thinking something over.

This made Valerie nervous.

"Excuse me for asking this, Agent Law," the doctor finally said. "But your first name is Valerie, isn't it?"

"Yes. Is this an issue?"

"It's just," he said, hesitating. "The patient you've asked to see, she has a daughter named Valerie Law. I know this because she talks about her. And she is an FBI agent. I also know that the patient doesn't want to see her daughter."

Valerie nodded knowingly in response.

"So, you can see why I find it unusual that a request comes in from an FBI agent to see her and I notice the name?"

"I'm not going to insult your intelligence, Doctor," Valerie said. "I am Gwen Law's daughter."

The doctor raised an eyebrow and said: "Are you here in an official capacity, then? It certainly sounded like it in your emails."

Valerie had to think quick. She had used her FBI credentials to petition for a meeting with her mother, but she had to link that to her work, and there was only one way to do that.

"Have you ever heard of the Criminal Psychopathy Unit at Quantico, Doctor?"

"No, I haven't."

"It's a relatively new unit," Valerie explained. "It was set up six months ago. We're looking at violent, psychopathic behaviors, and we're using our insights to track down the country's most dangerous fugitives."

"Ah, wait a minute," he said, smiling. "The Bone Ripper case, that was you, wasn't it? That was all over the news, but they only mentioned the name of the new unit in passing."

"Yes," Valerie said. " That's us. We concluded that case a couple of months ago."

"Doctor Will Cooper was injured during the arrest, wasn't he? I remember now. I was surprised to hear that he was on an actual in-field investigation. Given that he's an academic. I've meet him a few times at conferences on abnormal psychology. How is he?"

"He's better," Valerie said. "As brilliant as ever, though don't tell him I told you that." Valerie laughed, hoping that her friendly approach would gain her some leeway.

"I'd love to pick your brains about some of the cases you've been working on," the doctor said.

"That would be good," Valerie said, unsure if he was actually interested professionally or hitting on her. His body language was difficult to read. "On the matter of my mother…"

"Yes, so, Agent Law…"

"Valerie, please," she said, hoping to keep things amicable.

"I am still puzzled why you're here… I hate to ask, but you're not using your position with the Bureau to gain access to her, are you?"

"No, of course not," she answered, feeling the lie stick in the back of her throat. Valerie was always a straight shooter. She didn't like to deceive, but her mother's well-being was at stake, not to mention some family business that had to be cleared up. It felt to Valerie as though her mother's mental state was somehow deeply connected to the pieces of paper she had sent, scrawled in wild handwriting.

She both wanted the truth and to help her mom. But she would keep that to herself, for now.

"Then, if I may ask, why *are* you here?" The doctor waited for an answer.

"Gwen Law has a history of psychotic violence." Valerie kept her cool.

"Brought on by significant impairment due to her mental condition, Agent Law. That's why she's here after all. She's a victim as much as you were."

Valerie bristled at that comment.

"I'm sorry," the doctor continued. "I'm intimately familiar with your mother's case as someone treating her, and I know what you underwent. The attack with the knife when you were a child when your mother was caught in her delusions... That somehow she had to cut the evil out of you."

Valerie could feel her eyelids flicker. The emotion of those memories was always there. Always.

The doctor continued: "So, I guess what I'm saying is, I understand why someone from your unit might be interested in speaking with her for research purposes, but it seems highly inappropriate that it be you, her daughter. I would have rejected the request immediately, but I have to say I am curious as to your reasoning."

"It's a unique scenario where the interviewer is a victim of the person's crimes," Valerie said, improvising. "Our unit wants to know if anything can be gleaned from her reaction to this. And whether my presence will affect her answers."

"It seems highly irregular…"

"It is, Doctor. But that's what we deal with every day. The highly irregular." Valerie took a chance, she stood up. "Of course, if you feel it's an ethical breach, I'll be on my way and my colleague Agent Carlson can come for the interview."

The doctor seemed off balance at the suggestion. "No, no, that's not necessary. On one condition, however. Would you share your findings with me?"

"Yes, that would be fine."

"And a meeting to hear about some of your investigations and what they can teach the profession about helping the criminally insane?" the doctor said, his eyes wide like a wolf ready for his supper.

"As long as it doesn't breach confidentiality, then yes, that would be acceptable. A professional meeting." Valerie emphasized that last point.

"Great!" the doctor said, standing up and rubbing his hands together. "If you'll follow me, then."

CHAPTER TWO

They walked through another security gate and then to Ward 8, where Valerie knew her mother was being kept. The Wakefield Psychiatric Hospital was a real mixed bag. Half prison, half healing environment. The decor, jumping from sterile white walls gave the impression that it was more of a hospital, but the occasional iron barred doors gave away its real purpose.

The patients, including Valerie's mother, were all highly violent, and some of them with long-term, court-ordered sentences.

"Are you ready?" Doctor Mellor asked, stopping at one of several locked doors.

Valerie nodded, but deep down she wasn't ready. She could never be.

The doctor unlocked the door and stepped inside. Valerie followed. This was the moment. The first time she had laid eyes on her mother for many years.

The sight was like a punch to the gut.

The room was dim.

"She doesn't like the bright lights," Doctor Mellor said quietly. "She suffers from hypersensitivity to stimuli, so we keep things quiet as best we can and the lights at a minimum."

Valerie didn't answer. She was too busy looking at her mother. The shell of the woman who once raised her.

She was a woman in her fifties, but her wild, unkempt black and gray hair made her look older. Dark patches beneath her eyes made her look sleep deprived, and the visible veins in her arms and forehead showed her emaciation.

Valerie could barely hold it together. She let out a quiet sob as she said: "Hi Mom." It was almost a whisper. A heartfelt whisper that could have come from a child, but Valerie knew that we are all children when interacting with our parents, no matter how old.

There was a silence. The doctor turned to the door. "I'll be right outside." He left, and the room seemed to grow somewhat dimmer to Valerie, but she knew it was in her mind.

"Mom," she said, stepping forward.

"Mom?" Gwen answered, raising her head and looking at Valerie.

Valerie smiled, tears running down her cheeks.

"It's me, Val."

"Val?" Gwen said, tilting her head to the side, considering her daughter. "I don't know a Val."

That cut deep. Valerie hadn't faced her mother in years. She had thought about what she would say to her, about how she'd balance out the good with the bad. How could Valerie reconcile her memories of her mother's kindness with those terrifying moments during her breakdown?

"I'm your daughter, Mom," Valerie said quietly. "I've come to see how you're doing."

"Doing... Doing... Doing..." Gwen repeated this over and over like a scratched record. "How am I doing?"

Valerie was shocked at how far gone her mother was. She was clearly heavily medicated, and it seemed like she was in the throes of some psychotic episode where memories and the world around her didn't register as they should have.

"I don't know you," Gwen said leaning back into her bed, propping herself up against the back wall. Her wild hair drooped over her face.

Valerie put her hand in her pocket and pulled out the folded sheet of paper her mother had sent. It was covered in scribbled handwriting. What perturbed Valerie the most about the writing, was that it contained several mentions of her father, a man she hadn't seen for years.

The words intimated something about him. Something that related to the work Valerie now did as an FBI profiler. She had to know what her mother meant. In her heart, she feared something terrible that would bring the fragile world she had built for herself, crashing to the ground.

And yet she still searched for the meaning behind the words.

"Mom," she said, holding the paper up. "Why did you send this to Suzie and ask her to give it to me?"

Gwen didn't reply. She stared, her eyes almost glazed over.

"Suzie said this was meant for me, Mom," Valerie continued. "Why did you send it?"

Valerie pointed at one of the scrawled sentences on the page and read it aloud: "The devil is inside you. I knew it when you were born. It's only a matter of time. Your father knew, but you'll never find him."

Gwen started to laugh. It twisted into a cackle. She leaned forward, her eyes wide and bulging. "The devil *is* inside... I'll cut it out of you!" She rushed forward at Valerie, but a restraint tied to the bed pulled Gwen back onto it. "I'll cut it out!"

Those words flashed in Valerie's mind. She felt her pulse quicken. A sickness grew in her stomach. She remembered being a child, her mother holding the knife above her saying those very same words.

The room began to spin, and Valerie found herself pounding on the door begging to be let out, all while her mother laughed and writhed in the darkness.

As Doctor Mellor opened the door, Valerie rushed out and raced along the corridor towards the exits.

"Agent Law!" Doctor Mellor yelled in the background. But she didn't respond.

The devil is in you, too, Valerie thought. *It's only a matter of time until I end up in a straightjacket.*

Valerie felt paper thin. Like she could be torn in two by the forces in her life. She'd done so well to hold the horrors of her past at bay, but now they were coming for her.

And at the worst time: She was about to embark on a trip with her boyfriend Tom. A trip that would require her to smile and act normal as she met his parents for the first time. They would not accept her if they knew her inner turmoil if they knew her past.

Valerie felt she was *anything* but normal, and she feared that her anxieties would build and come out at the worst moment. A moment that the very survival of her personal relationship with Tom hinged upon.

CHAPTER THREE

Valerie exited the plane, the sunlight above scattering between the clouds. Tom appeared alongside her. This was the biggest step she'd ever taken in a relationship. A trip to see her boyfriend's family.

She had always kept people at arm's length, mainly because of her own family's volatile past. This wasn't a step she took lightly. But Tom was worth it.

Valerie took a deep breath of the Indiana air, and headed into the airport.

Tom squeezed her hand reassuringly. "You feeling okay? You seem pretty tense."

"Yeah," Valerie said. "I'm fine. Just nervous."

"You don't need to be," Tom said, his voice soothing. "My parents are going to love you."

Not if they knew, Tom, Valerie thought. *Not if they knew your girlfriend could end up in an institution.*

It had been a couple of weeks since Valerie had visited her mom, but even with the change of scenery, Valerie couldn't shake the encounter from her mind.

Worse, she couldn't shake her mother's words. Her mom was sick. Her sister had the same mental illness, or at least a similar one. Valerie felt the struggle inside of herself to keep things together. A struggle she feared she would lose one day, just like they had.

"Tom!" a cheery voice said loudly as they exited the airport.

"Dad!" Tom ran up and hugged his father. His dad was very much like him, tall, athletic, and bookish at the same time, though about 25 years older. Valerie had an even clearer idea now of what Tom would look like in the coming decades.

"Well, Tom," his dad said looking at Valerie. "You've sold her short. You said she was beautiful, but that was an understatement. I think you're punching above your weight."

Valerie took the compliment and smiled. In other hands it could have come off as sleazy or inappropriate. But it just sounded like a typical dad joke. Not that she had much experience of having a father in her life.

"It's lovely to meet you," Valerie said.

"Please, call me Mark," he said, shaking Valerie's hand.

Mark led Valerie to his car in the parking lot outside of Indianapolis's main airport. "Here she is."

"You're still driving this old thing?" Tom said, laughing.

The green station wagon was a relic from the past. But Valerie could tell it had been looked after. It was comforting in a way to her. A link to a different time.

"Dad you used to drive me to school in this old thing," Tom said. "I was mortified."

"I like it," Valerie smiled, getting into the back seat.

"She has taste," Mark observed. "In cars at least."

Tom laughed. There was clearly no malice in Mark joking with his son. It was a way for them to communicate. Valerie had read some interesting studies about male bonding and how humor was a critical component of it. But for now, she was trying to put her insights into behavior to the side.

The drive to the sleepy suburb of Oakston in the south of the city was a mix of questions and jokes. Valerie was on her best behavior She could mix it with the best, but when trying to make a good impression, she knew she had to pull back the darker side of her humor.

She knew that she'd developed her sense of humor as a way to cope with her childhood trauma, and this had only become more important as she faced the horrors of tracking down serial killers for a living. *You'll either laugh or you'll cry.* Something an uncle had once told her.

She tried to choose laughter, but it wasn't always easy. Not with her past. Not with her work, either.

The unfamiliar roads of Indianapolis passed by as Mark drove at an increasingly slow rate.

"Dad," Tom said. "We can get out and walk if you'd like, so it would be quicker?"

"Speed kills, Son."

"So does boredom."

"I like it," Valerie interjected. "A nice scenic driver."

Tom and Mark laughed. "Not too scenic," Mark explained. "We're only a few minutes from the house. In fact, here we are."

They turned onto a picturesque street with manicured lawns. Valerie shuddered inside. It was so clean. So wholesome. Everything her family life was not.

The car slowed even more as they reached the end of the road.

The door to a large townhouse opened up as soon as Tom's dad parked in its long driveway.

It revealed a middle aged woman with a round, kind face. She was dressed immaculately in a flowery dress, and had a sense of home about her. She beckoned excitedly to them.

Valerie felt a dark pang in her stomach. Something occurred to her as she left the car. Tom's family was a reminder of everything hers was not.

"Valerie!" the woman said walking down the steps with open arms. She threw them around Valerie and gave her a big hug. "It's so lovely to finally meet you. I'm Hannah, and while you're here, I want you to feel right at home. Come on."

She patted Tom on the cheek and took Valerie's hand, leading her up the stairs and into the house.

CHAPTER FOUR

Fate had a way of finding Valerie, at least, that's what Charlie thought. Jackson Weller was on the other end of the phone explaining that he hadn't been able to get in touch with Valerie.

His words were grim and tense, undercut by the sound of Charlie's kids playing out in the backyard.

It was a beautiful sunny day. Charlie was at home with his wife and two kids. It was supposed to be his down time. The time every FBI agent needs to keep their private life in order.

But that order was about to be put on hold.

"You can't get Valerie?" Charlie asked, holding the phone. The smell of the barbecue from the back lawn hung in the air.

"Not yet," said Jackson. "I know she's on vacation with Tom, and I hate to interrupt…"

"But you're going to anyway?" Charlie asked.

There was a silence.

"Chief," said Charlie, always using that term affectionately. "Val is having a pretty rough time. It won't affect her job performance, but I think we should at least give her some peace. At least until her vacation is over."

"We've got another killer," Jackson said, somberly. "It's come down the wire to us. The murders are violent, targeting women of the same age, and showing possible escalation. I'm not certain they are connected, but I think there's a real possibility it's the same killer, and we could be looking at the beginning of a killing spree. This is what the Criminal Psychopathy Unit at Quantico was designed to do, catch the killer before they add another victim to their list. I need this evaluated and then followed up on, immediately."

Charlie sighed.

He was worried about Valerie. He knew that she had been trying to reconnect with both her parents recently, and that was putting a lot of pressure on her.

He watched his two kids running around on the grass outside. They were playing with water pistols, screaming in delight as they soaked each other beneath the golden blanket of the sun.

He couldn't imagine ever hurting them. Valerie had been through hell with her parents, her father running out on her when she was a kid, and then her mother's violent breakdown.

"Jackson," Charlie said, quietly. "How about we start this case with just me and Will. We'll go over the initial investigation. We can let Val get her down time and come back stronger."

"Do you think she needs it?" Jackson asked.

"Everyone needs it, Chief. Besides, she's actually staying not far from the murder scenes, so if we need her, we can bring her in quickly."

There was a pause and then Jackson said: "Okay. Let Will do most of the profiling, but keep him right."

"I will. Thanks."

Charlie hung up the phone. As he did, his wife, Angela came into the house from the backyard.

She didn't even have to ask. She just looked at him.

"Not again, Charlie."

"I have to, Angela," he said. "It's either me or Val. And she's on holiday."

"So are you."

"Yeah," said Charlie. "That's true. But you know Val is going through a lot, and I've already had a few days with the kids."

"So how long will you be gone?" Angela said, her voice frustrated.

"I'm not sure," answered Charlie. "Two women in their twenties have been murdered. The Bureau requested we take a look at it in case it's the beginning of a killing spree. I'll know more once I've assessed the situation. I'm sorry, Honey…"

Angela sighed. "You can be the one to break it to the kids."

"I will," Charlie said. "I'll need to pack my suitcase as well. We're flying out to Indianapolis in a couple of hours. Any chance of packing me something to eat? You know I hate airline food."

"In your dreams," Angela said walking out of the room. Then came her voice in the distance. "I'll make you a sandwich."

Charlie opened the door to the backyard. His kids were in full flow, laughing and playing. Georgina was only three, so it wouldn't affect her as much. But Richard was five, and he was starting to ask more and more questions about why his dad was away for days, sometimes weeks at a time.

"I should have picked a different career," Charlie said under his breath as he walked up to his two kids in the sun and gave them both a hug.

CHAPTER FIVE

Charlie gripped his glass tightly as the plane shuddered. They had hit a storm, the plane dipping up and down occasionally in the turbulence. This wasn't a problem for Charlie. He'd served in the army for years before becoming an FBI agent. Bad flights were an occupational hazard.

It was his friend and colleague, Doctor Will Cooper, who seemed unnerved.

Will sat next to Charlie, pulling at his shirt collar with his finger to let in some air, while sporadically grabbing hold of the armrest of his chair.

"You okay, Will?" Charlie asked with a smile. "Couldn't you prescribe yourself something to make the flight a little less eventful?"

"You know very well I'm not that type of a doctor," Will said, wiping perspiration from his brow.

"I'm just messing around," Charlie said, finishing his drink. "What's that?" Charlie looked out of the window at one of the wings moving in the wind and rain.

"Dear Lord, what?" Will said, moving forward.

Charlie patted Will on the back. "Oh wait, it's just the wing."

"Very good," Will sniped, not happy at his colleague's jokes.

Charlie had flown so many times he'd forgotten what it was like to be nervous. He decided to do the decent thing and help his friend keep his mind off the weather.

He pointed at a brown envelope in front of him. "Have you looked at this yet?"

"Yes," Will said, clearing his throat. "Two homicides. Both women in their twenties. Quite brutal."

"Any idea of a profile for the killer yet?"

"It's still too early," Will said. " Statistically speaking, a killer like this is usually a white man in his thirties or forties. Most probably with social issues, difficulty fitting in. He probably hasn't killed before this or at least no one has reported any murders linked to him."

"Okay," Charlie said, pressing his lips together. The doctor wasn't really giving Charlie anything he didn't already know, but it was good for him to talk a bit to keep his mind off the plane as it struggled through the storm.

Will continued: "If he's currently homicidal and in a period of escalation, he'll need to kill again. The murders will become more brutal as he attempts to elicit his own arousal."

"You think there's a sexual element, then?"

"Not necessarily," said Will. "While there is often a violent sexual element to such killings, sometimes by 'arousal' we mean a sense of power. It could also be a way for the killer to vent anger, frustration, or even to strike out at women who are similar to someone who has wronged him."

"A lot of options for a profile, then," Charlie mused.

"Yes," agreed Will. "We'll know more once we look at things in greater detail. The murder scene, the bodies, etc."

Charlie flicked through the file and landed on one of the crime scene photos. Blood was everywhere. He hated how desensitized he had become to such scenes. Between the horrors he'd seen during his tours, and now the violent deaths he had investigated as part of the Criminal Psychopathy Unit, it took a lot to shock him. Too much.

"It's a shame Valerie isn't here," Will said. "She is brilliantly insightful, even at such an early stage."

"I'll try and not take that personally, Doc."

"Oh no," Will said, his cheeks flushing red. "You are always integral, Charlie. I just mean it's better when all three of us are here."

Charlie patted Will on the arm. "You're okay, Will. It takes a lot to get under my skin. Besides, maybe it'll do us some good to spend some time working together just the two of us. You and Valerie have done that before."

"Ah," Will said, brightly. "Right you are. Like a male bonding experience?"

Charlie sighed. He liked Will a lot, but he always had to verbally reaffirm whatever psychological theory was in his head, and sometimes Charlie wished he'd just relax.

"Sure, Will. But let's not openly call it that," he said, laughing. That laugh didn't last long. Will turned the page on the file and saw another angle of the crime scene. More blood. More death. Charlie wondered if it would ever stop. Would there ever be a time when violent killers no longer existed?

He'd gladly be out of a job then.

19

Will was looking at the photo in Charlie's hand.

"You know, I have a theory about this case."

"I thought you said it was too early for a profile?" Charlie observed.

Will nodded. "That's true, but there's an uncomfortable coincidence I wanted to talk about. The first murder just outside of Indianapolis took place shortly after the closure of the Wendel Institute."

"The Wendel Institute?" Charlie asked, intrigued.

"Yes," said Will. The plane bumped again and he patted his brow until things were smoother.

"It's not going to fall out of the sky, Will," Charlie said, half cynically, half supportive.

"Quite," said Will. "The Wendel Institute was an experimental psychiatric ward that had been running for the last 16 years. It lost funding due to a controversy over their methods recently and was shut down."

Charlie moved forward in his seat. "Violent patients?"

"It's possible."

"And what happened to them after the place shut down?"

"Well," said Will. "Some of the patients were cut adrift from any treatment. They were let out. Of course, those running the Wendel Institute claimed that they were all fully processed and no longer a danger to themselves or others. But there has been some debate about that."

"Interesting," Charlie said. He sat momentarily in deep thought. Coincidences happened all the time, but as an FBI agent who hunted violent killers, he knew never to take a coincidence for granted. It could always lead to a catch, and that was all he ever wanted: to catch them before they could kill again.

"I thought it was worth mentioning as the dates lined up," Will offered.

"Considering we don't have many leads yet, Will, I think it's great. When did you hear about this?"

"Just the other day, I have an old colleague who works… worked at the Wendel Institute. The fact that, as far as we know, the killings started soon after all of those patients were released…"

"Our killer could be among them," Charlie said, finishing Will's thought. "How many patients were at that Wendel Institute?"

"I don't know the exact number," Will explained. "But it could have been more than a hundred."

"We're going to need more help," Charlie said, grimly. He took his cellphone out of his pocket, scrolled through his numbers and stopped at the letter V.

"She's on vacation, Charlie," Will said. "Maybe we should try to handle this ourselves."

Charlie paused for a moment. He wanted Valerie to have a break from it all. He knew she needed it. But Will's revelation about the Wendel Institute complicated things. They'd need her to help identify potential suspects out of those patients.

He also knew she'd be mad if he didn't tell her about the case.

"I'll just tell her that we'll be nearby," Charlie said. "Then... Whether she joins us or not is up to her... It's a good thing I paid for some Wi-Fi. "

The plane struggled again in the storm as Charlie hit the call button on his messenger app and dialed Valerie's number.

CHAPTER SIX

It wasn't until dessert was served that Valerie felt truly uncomfortable. The table, set in a large dining room within Tom's family home, had been crammed with roast beef and enough vegetables, gravy, and mashed potatoes to feed all four of them many times over. Now they were making way for some pecan pie.

It was delicious, but as Valerie scooped out some more with her spoon, the inevitable happened. The question that she had been dreading the entire visit inevitably came.

"So, tell me about your parents," Hannah said over the table, smiling, playing with a golden necklace around her neck.

Valerie could feel it. Tom was tensing up. She knew he had been dreading that too, though he had never told her.

Valerie took a deep breath and tried to think of the most diplomatic way to put it. She was scared that they would think she came from a bad place, that she was somehow not good enough for Tom.

Deep down, she just never liked facing her past. It was why she did everything she could to avoid questions like that.

"My father left us when I was a kid," Valerie said, quietly.

"Oh, dear," Tom's father said. "I'm so sorry to hear that, Valerie." He continued to cut into a side of beef.

"What about your mother?" Hannah asked. "And your sister? I'm sure Tom mentioned you had one."

That irked Valerie, although she knew it shouldn't have. She didn't like anyone discussing her family, but she knew Tom probably skirted over it as best he could with his parents. And they were bound to ask a lot about the woman their son had kept going on about and never met.

That included her past, too.

"My mother…" Valerie said, trailing off.

There was a heavy silence and Valerie felt caught in a spiral of emotions. Tom's family, so perfect, so pristine, and her own, a psychotic mess. A mess that had infected every part of her life and, if she wasn't careful, would push through and bring her own sanity to the brink.

And yet she still didn't say anything. For some reason a clock ticking somewhere sounded louder before, each tick passing by like an echo from some distant place.

"Valerie's mother isn't well," Tom finally said.

Valerie turned towards him, angry. "Tom, don't say that."

"I'm just trying to explain that you don't see your mom because she's not well, and it's complicated."

"I'd rather we just talk about something else, if everyone doesn't mind," Valerie said.

"Of course, of course," Mark said. "No need to press. Your business is your business, Valerie." He smiled and then went back to chomping through his dinner like it was his last meal.

There was another silence again, and the ticking clock kept going, kept ticking.

Each time it did, it was like a thorn in Valerie's mind. She looked around at Tom's family and felt it coming. *What's this?* she thought. *A heart attack? Am I dying?*

But no, she knew what it was. It was a panic attack. All the stress of seeing her mother and trying to switch between her cases and Tom, it was all bubbling up now.

It swelled inside of her like a maelstrom until her hands started shaking.

She knew she had to get out of there before she had a full on meltdown. And then what would Tom's family have thought of her? She stood up, breathing quickly.

"I... I need to get some air. I'll be right back..."

"Are you okay?" Hannah asked.

But Valerie didn't answer. She was already out of the room, rushing down the hallway and then out into the fresh air.

"Breathe," Valerie said to herself. "Just breathe... Let it pass..."

She took a deep breath and felt her body shudder slightly from the adrenaline passing through it.

Slowly, surely, her breathing settled down, and she began to calm. The world stopped spinning. It became stark and real.

She heard something behind her. It was a familiar sound. Tom appeared through the front door holding Valerie's phone.

"Are you okay?" Tom asked.

"I'm sorry, Tom," Valerie said. "I shouldn't have come. I don't know what to do with myself right now. It's like I'm falling and I don't know when I'll stop."

"I'm here."

"You always are, and I love you for it."

Tom looked down at the phone in his hand and sighed. "It's Charlie. You better answer it."

Valerie took the phone and answered it, steadying her breathing. "Hey, Charlie. What's up?" She did her best to sound normal.

"Sorry, Val, I know you're on your vacation," Charlie said. "But we've got a big case here, and I wanted to run a few ideas past you. It's also in the vicinity of where you're staying, so, it's totally up to you, but..."

"Send me the deets," Valerie said. "I'll be there. Let me get back to you, Charlie." She hung up.

"What?" Tom said, his voice filled with disbelief.

"Charlie has sent me a case. It's in and around Indianapolis, I think. He needs my help." Valerie knew it was more than that. She didn't feel exactly ready for another case, but it was preferential than having to spend the days ahead putting on a fake smile with Tom's family.

She liked them, but she didn't have it in her to cover over the cracks like that.

"Valerie," Tom said. "We just got here. My mom spent hours preparing all this food."

"I know," Valerie replied. "But they need me. I *will* come back here, Tom. Just give me a couple of days. I'll explain to your family that..."

"Don't bother," Tom said, turning towards the house. "Just call me when you need me. But don't freeze me out. I'm not sure I can take it, Val."

Valerie lifted her hand to rub his back, but Tom moved forward and said, "Do you need a car?"

"No," Valerie answered. "I'll call the Bureau and they'll get one dropped off."

Valerie moved into the house and back into the dining room. "I'm sorry, Hannah, Mark," Valerie said. "But I've just received a call from the FBI. I'm needed for a day or two to consult on a case not far from here."

Hannah seemed shocked. "I hope I didn't offend you... I..."

"No, please, you mustn't think that," Valerie said. "You've been so kind to me today. And I will be back here soon, I promise."

"Okay, Dear," Mark said.

But Valerie could tell he was a bit put out.

Valerie left the room and put the call into the bureau. The car would be dropped off within the hour. Just long enough for Valerie to feel caught in two minds about whether she was doing the right thing or not.

You're not ready for a case right now, a voice in her head said. She knew it was right. But she didn't intend on listening to it.

"I'm really sorry Tom," Valerie said, leaning down and kissing Tom on the cheek.

"Just be safe," he said. But he didn't look at her.

Valerie said goodbye to his parents, grabbed some of her things from the car, and then waited outside for her ride. A car that would take her on another brutal chase to catch a psychopath.

But this time, she felt somewhere deep inside, that such a case might finally push her over the edge, a push that would end with joining her sister and mother in the halls and rooms of a psychiatric ward.

CHAPTER SEVEN

Valerie had been waiting for an hour and a half outside of the Ringwind Motel. As places went, it was a little more upmarket than the usual motels she found herself in. The FBI's budget usually only stretched to the cheapest accommodation, and that meant cheap drinks and cheap beds in equal measure.

But the Ringwind Motel was looked after by an elderly couple, the Makins. And they seemed to care for the place with genuine pride. That made a difference.

Valerie breathed in the warm air. Autumn was coming, but the summer wasn't quite done with the world just yet. She stared at the parking lot and wondered if her partners would be surprised to see her.

She was surprised to be there herself. She understood how hurt Tom was that she left so quickly, but she'd make it up to him. She had to.

A rental Ford drove into the parking lot, turned, and then parked almost immediately in front of Valerie's recently acquired room.

Charlie practically leapt out of the driver's side.

"What the hell are you doing here?"

"Thought you boys could use some help," Valerie smiled.

Will exited from the passenger's side. He walked up to Valerie and gave her a hug. "I'm glad to see you, Valerie. But I had hoped you would give yourself a little more time to…"

"To cool off?" Valerie said. "No… There's too much that needs to be done, Will. Besides, I really do feel rested. Really."

For a moment, she felt the eyes of her two friends on her. She saw a flicker of sadness in them. Sadness and disbelief. They didn't believe her, she could tell that much. Though neither Charlie nor Will said it.

Charlie walked around to the rear of the car and grabbed his bags, Will did the same. "It's still early enough. Will we check in and then head to the crime scene?"

"Sure," said Valerie. "I still need to get acquainted with the case."

"Here," Will said, digging into his bag. "This is the file Jackson sent over."

"Great," Valerie said, looking at it. "I have a digital copy, but I much prefer studying it in person."

"Will already has a lead," Charlie said, putting his bags on the ground.

"Oh?" Valerie said. She was happy about the lead, though she felt a little out of the loop.

"A controversial psychiatric hospital called the Wendel Institute was shut down a few days before the murders started."

Valerie shook her head. "Don't tell me someone was released who shouldn't have been?"

"I'm not sure, yet," said Will. "But I have a friend who worked there, and they were concerned about some patients and their readiness to go back into the community. Especially considering that some of them had been under intense treatment for violent impulses."

"I think it's worth looking at," said Charlie. "We might get lucky."

"Definitely," said Valerie thoughtfully. "Let's get you two settled in and we'll head to the crime scene. Will, could you phone your friend and find out who we need to contact to get access to the patient list for the Wendel Institute?"

"Absolutely."

As Charlie and Will walked to the reception to check in, Valerie could feel it: The stress of her argument with Tom was slowly moving to the back of her mind. For a moment, she considered how unhealthy it all was. She needed her job. She needed a case. If she had that, she didn't need to face her life and the problems within it.

She wondered if deep down, she needed there to be murder in the world to feel worth something.

That was a crazy idea, but then mental illness was rife in her family. Perhaps it began when such thoughts felt reasonable.

CHAPTER EIGHT

The barn looked familiar to Charlie. It looked like every serene country painting he had ever seen. But this was not a serene place. Not now that a body lay inside and several police officers were standing guard.

Police tape wrapped around the old wooden building, keeping the public away. But then, there wasn't any public to speak of. The barn was on a lonely piece of field, surrounded by yellow grass and thorny bushes.

"You wouldn't think such a thing could happen in a place like this," Will said looking around.

But Charlie had seen it all. In combat. On the streets. In people's homes. Death could come from anywhere and at any time.

Valerie walked quickly in front of Charlie. She had seen something on the ground. She took out a pen from her pocket and lifted a few blades of dead grass with it.

"What's that?" asked Will.

"There's cut grass here," Valerie answered. "It looks out of place."

"It is," said Charlie. He knew how to track people. He knew the tell-tale signs. He traced the small patch of uncut grass to an almost indiscernible depression in the ground.

"You found something else, Charlie?" Valerie asked.

"The woman was dragged up here," Charlie said. "Going by the crime scene photos and how much blood was in the barn, she must have been unharmed at that point. But those cut blades of grass came from her shoes. And they don't belong here. The grass is a different species."

Charlie stood up, took a photo of the depression and the cut grass blades, and then walked with Valerie and Will into the barn.

The smell of blood was unmistakable. That meant it was fresh. The barn was dim inside, save for the occasional shard of light that slipped between the warped wooden slats.

Looking around, Charlie saw pieces of old rusted farm machinery leaning against the walls. Weeds and other invasive plants cropped up intermittently through the soil floor.

"This place hasn't been used in years," Charlie said.

"Yeah," replied Valerie. "The officer I spoke to said that the owner of the land died five years ago and there's been a dispute ever since between his children about who owns this place."

"Families. Can't always pick them," Will remarked.

Charlie felt Valerie bristle slightly.

Will looked at Charlie in response, momentarily. Charlie nodded back while Valerie began to climb an old wooden ladder to a partial second floor.

They both knew what that look meant. They both knew Valerie was struggling with her family.

Valerie disappeared up onto the second floor that jutted halfway out from the barn wall.

"You better come up here." She sounded solemn. And when Valerie Law sounded solemn, Charlie knew she was looking at something terrible.

Charlie went up second. The ladder creaked, but it held his weight. As he reached the upper floor, he saw what had affected Valerie so acutely.

A single metal chain dropped down about fifteen feet from an iron beam which ran along the ceiling. The chain moved slightly in an unseen draft. Hanging from it, was the body of a woman. Her hands were bound with what looked like cord, and her neck was wrapped in the chain.

Her face was purple, but the body was fresh enough. The stench of death that Charlie had so often become accustomed to was not yet prevalent. The blood, however, more than made up for that.

Beneath the body was a small trough used to feed animals. It had caught the woman's blood, which had poured from several gaping wounds in her neck and chest.

"Can someone give me a hand?" Will said, panting from the ladder.

Charlie bent over and pulled Will up.

"Prepare yourself, Will," Charlie said.

Will straightened up when he saw the poor woman.

Having solved several cases now, Charlie knew that Will was getting used to this sort of thing, but he was still more fragile to it than Valerie and Charlie.

Will covered his mouth with a handkerchief as he approached the body.

Valerie was looking at the wounds on her body.

"We won't know until there's an autopsy," she said. "But the wounds don't look planned. Looks like some sort of implement was used, but not a knife."

"Looks like the victim was killed in a fit of rage," Charlie observed, stepping closer. "That chain is the only thing holding her up, and it's wrapped haphazardly around her neck. Looks like whoever did this, did it in a hurry."

"Yes, but why?" Will said. "This location is out of the way, so they surely didn't think they'd be disturbed?"

"It's a sloppy murder," Valerie said. "Logically, they had time here to do what they wanted. But it's so all over the place… The killer must have panicked."

"That would suggest the killer didn't plan to do this," Charlie mused. "Could he have pulled her inside here without knowing what he was really going to do?"

"Yes, Charlie," Will agreed. "That would make sense. He drags the girl in here. Then, he ties her up. She's seen too much. Perhaps she's even seen his face. And then…"

"He grabs a piece of farm equipment," Charlie said. "A tool that was lying around."

"Hmm," said Valerie thoughtfully.

Charlie knew that meant she didn't fully agree.

"What are you thinking, Valerie?" asked Will.

Valerie pointed at the trough and then looked over the side of the flooring. She didn't say anything as she peered around. Suddenly, she pointed in the corner.

"Look over there," she said. "The imprints on the ground."

Charlie walked over and took a look. Sure enough, there were markings in the corner. He turned and looked at the body again, the poor woman's blood drained into the trough.

"He brought the trough up here," he said, coldly.

"Yes," said Valerie. "But why? That would have taken too much time considering how heavy it was. Was it just to cover up the blood or is there a symbolic reason?"

"Perhaps," answered Will.

Charlie's mind was running through the possibilities. One such possibility stuck out like a thorn. It was a memory he had of an earlier case he'd been on.

"Did I ever mentioned the Freddy Henley case to you, Val?"

30

"No."

"It was before we were partners. He killed a guy in cold blood, but when the blood poured onto him, he freaked. We found him a blubbering mess, admitting to everything. Turns out, he was a clean freak and couldn't handle human blood touching him."

"Ah!" Valerie said, getting the drift. "So, you're saying the killer could be some sort of obsessive compulsive who brought the trough up here because he was compelled to not make a mess?"

"Maybe," Charlie replied. "It's just a theory."

"A good one," Will interjected. "That would explain why, even though he was in a hurry, he took the time to bring the trough up here. His compulsive cleanliness overrode his anxiety about getting caught, at least temporarily."

Charlie felt slight shame in being pleased that his colleagues recognized his efforts. Shame because, though he had to take some pride in his work to be good at it and save lives, it was a pride that was only made possible because an innocent woman had been butchered. He'd have traded it all in for the woman to open her eyes and be alive. But those eyes were never going to be opened.

"Wait!" Charlie said. "Her eyes are closed."

"So the killer closed them," Will said, quietly.

"I've seen that before," Valerie stated. "It usually means there is some sort of remorse."

"Or connection to the victim," Will added.

"We need to ID the body," Charlie said. "Then we can see if she had any connection to the first victim."

"Maria…" Valerie said, trailing off as if losing her train of thought.

"Maria Johansson," Will offered.

It was strange to Charlie that Valerie couldn't remember the name of the first victim. She was always so on point. But he could see it in her eyes. The sleeplessness. The anxiety. Something was weighing her down, and Charlie was convinced it was to do with her family.

"I did read the file," Valerie said. "She was murdered outside a hospital. Similar age to this victim. A brutal attack, but nothing like this, being strung up…"

"I wonder why Jackson gave the case to us; he seemed to be sure this was the work of the same killer when I spoke with him," Will said.

No one replied. All that could be heard were the creaking beams of wood around them, and the quiet rattle of the chain as it moved slowly back and forward, swinging the body a few inches back and forward.

31

"Maybe we should query it?" Charlie said. "It could be different killers. Val?"

Valerie didn't say anything, she was looking at the victim's face.

"Val?" Charlie asked again.

"Oh, sorry," she said, as if coming out of a daze. "The two victims look alike; we shouldn't overlook that. Sometimes the connection can be that simple."

But Valerie kept looking at the woman's face. Something was disturbing her, and Charlie knew it.

"Is everything okay, Val?" Charlie said, softly. "You know you can talk to us if something…"

"I'm fine," Valerie snapped. "Please. Just let it be… Let's speak with the cops outside and then get back to the motel. We can check in with the coroner as soon as she has something for us once the body has been removed."

Valerie moved over to the ladder and began descending. Will stepped forward towards Charlie as she disappeared back to the ground floor.

"She isn't herself," he whispered.

"I know," Charlie replied. "Let's keep an eye on her."

Charlie didn't dare ask more. He had a feeling that Will knew some things he didn't, but he didn't want to press him on it for fear of Valerie overhearing. Loyalty was a big thing to Valerie, this Charlie knew. If she thought they were discussing her private business, that wouldn't exactly go down well.

Charlie simply nodded to Will and then followed Valerie back down the ladder.

Once Will came down the ladder, the three investigators left the barn behind. Valerie moved off to talk with one of the on-scene police officers.

"We shouldn't have contacted her. Valerie should be on vacation with Tom. I think she needs the space," Will said.

"I don't know," Charlie said quietly. "I think there's more to this."

He watched his partner. There was something in the way she stood. Something in the way she held herself. Charlie had seen that look before during the war.

It was the look of someone trying desperately to hold themselves together.

CHAPTER NINE

The ceiling of the motel room mesmerized Valerie. It was a point of focus. A place she looked up at from her bed, her worried mind painting its blank white surface with memories and regrets.

Something had happened during the day at the crime scene. A woman brutally murdered, strung up by a chain like an animal at a slaughterhouse.

Valerie's professionalism usually allowed her to negotiate such terrible environments without it distracting her from her job. It was disrespectful to allow for distraction. For the memory of the victim and her family, she had to focus on catching the killer.

But the face of the murdered woman would not allow her an escape from distraction.

The nameless victim looked astonishingly like her sister, Suzie. And each time Valerie tried to close her eyes and go to sleep, she saw that face hanging with the chain wrapped around her neck.

Valerie was unsure if this was merely a product of her current familial situation. Suzie and her mother were constantly on her mind. Their sickness. Her mother's and sister's fractured minds a constant reminder that the same unstable mindset might be worming its way through her own brain.

Looking up at the motel ceiling, Valerie tried to steady her breathing. She tried to close her eyes and think of something else. But the face of the victim. The face of her sister. The face of her mother. These were sights that would not let her be.

And they would haunt her until morning when the coroner's office beckoned. When the identity of the woman would be revealed.

*

Valerie was exhausted. But she had to keep moving, keep working. She had been to too many coroners' offices throughout the years. This one was no different. It was another place filled with fluorescent light, cold air, and cold bodies.

She watched for a moment as Charlie took the lead, entering the mortuary with Will close behind.

"I've got to get myself back into the game," she thought to herself.

Valerie walked by Charlie and shook the hands of the coroner.

He was a small man with bright glasses and bright eyes behind them. A thick layer of gray hair on top of his head made him appear distinguished.

"I'm agent Law," Valerie said. "This is agent Carlson and Dr. Cooper an expert in the field of criminal psychopathy."

"It's a pleasure," the coroner said. "Just call me Hank, there's no need for second names here."

Valerie was grateful to not have to keep up airs and graces. She was too tired for that. "I'm Valerie, this is Charlie and Will."

The coroner nodded and then walked to the back of the room. On the rear wall there was a line of eight stainless steel doors reaching up to about waist height. Hank pulled open the third door, which clanked as it released its holding mechanism.

He pulled the tray on the bottom, grating slightly as it moved, rolling along on wheeled metal supports. On top of the tray lay a thin white sheet. Beneath that was, undoubtedly, the body of victim number two that had been found in the barn. It shook slightly as the trolley came to a rest.

The coroner pulled the sheet back slowly. Valerie observed that he showed more respect to the dead than some within his profession. But she didn't blame them. Seeing so many bodies numbs a person's emotional center, at least while they work.

The sheet peeled back revealing the same face that haunted Valerie during the night. The woman did resemble her sister Suzie, there was no doubt about that. But Valerie still wondered if her mind was playing tricks on her. That her wearied mind was seeing things that weren't there. Seeing things could have been the start of it all. The start of her slide into madness.

She did her best to shake the thought and pointed to several wounds on the girl's naked torso. "Hank, have you been able to identify the weapon that was used?"

Hank sighed. "It was most likely a tool grabbed from the barn. We found traces of rust on the wounds that was consistent with rust found on other equipment in the barn."

"Yeah, that's we figured," Charlie said. "Is there nothing more specific you can give us?"

"The wounds have a slight bend at the termination point," the coroner said. "You're probably looking for some sort of blade or cutting implement that is arched or curved. But without finding the specific murder weapon, it's impossible to tell. I would imagine the killer ditched it somewhere else."

"Nothing was recovered from the scene, unfortunately," Will offered.

Valerie thought back to the tools that she saw lying around the barn. She remembered the fields of thick grass that surrounded the place and mused about how the original founder of that barn, long since dead, would have had to deal with crops perhaps in a more traditional manner. Before the coming technological advancements. Before the bloodied hand of modernity.

"What about a scythe?" she asked.

"It's possible," the coroner said. "Although it would have to have been quite a small one. A large scythe can cut someone in two. These wounds are smaller than that."

"But you did say it was rusted?" Charlie asked. "Could a large scythe that had been blunted and rusted have caused the wounds?"

The coroner considered things for a moment. "It's possible."

Valerie turned to Charlie. "Get onto the local police department and ask them to be on the lookout for an old farming scythe. It could be a smaller single-handed one or a larger, full-sized and double-handed one."

"Sure," Charlie said, walking towards the exit.

"Oh," Will added. "It occurs to me that since the killer was in a hurry and perhaps didn't initially plan on killing the girl in the barn, he would have had to improvise the hiding place for the weapon. I doubt he would have taken it far with him."

"Yeah," Charlie agreed. "I think seeing someone carrying a scythe covered in blood would be pretty noticeable."

"What are you thinking, Will?" Valerie said, feeling that there was more to come from her colleague.

Will stood in contemplation for a moment, his glasses glinting in the fluorescent light from above.

"The killer may have been processing the kill emotionally afterwards," he said. "We already know that he closed the woman's eyes. If this was due to remorse, he may have been emotionally drawn to another place nearby. A place similar to the murder scene, but unstained by the kill."

"Do you mean," Valerie started. "That the killer may have been drawn to somewhere similar to the original barn. Almost like he would be erasing the kill? Going somewhere similar to the initial murder?"

"It's just a thought," Will said. "Highly speculative, but it would fit in with the remorse angle. And if he was in a hurried, unplanned mindset, he'd be governed more by emotion than intellect when trying to hide the weapon."

"Do you think," began Charlie," the killer would have gone back to another barn in the area and perhaps stashed the weapon there?"

"It's as good a theory as any," Valerie said. "Ask the local police department to furnish us with other known barns within a five-mile radius of the murder scene. Then get them to search those, if possible."

Charlie nodded and walked out of the room.

"Are you sure the killer was in a hurry?" the coroner asked. "It seems to me there was a level of planning to this. I mean if the killer used a scythe, that's got ritualistic harvesting connotations to it. Then there was the animal's trough filled with the victim's blood as well. That might be like a Satanic offering."

"Genuine Satanic killings are rare, Hank," Valerie said, knowing that if she didn't, Will would quite happily have given a lecture about Satanic panics throughout history and how they are almost always the product of hysteria.

"Do you think the location of the wounds on the victim's torso," Will asked, "are indicative of a panicked, rage induced attack? Or are the wounds slow and deliberate?"

"Well that's a point," Hank agreed. "The wounds are haphazard. In some cases, they're pretty shallow, which suggests the wounds were inflicted quickly, and violently. But you're right, it might suggest something more hurried like in your new theory."

Valerie looked down at the woman's body again. She couldn't help but stare at her face. The complexion was gray and lifeless, like plastic. But there was something about the chin and nose. *Suzie...* Valerie thought about her sister in that psychiatric ward. The same harsh fluorescent lighting hanging over her sister at the hospital as here, over the victim's naked body, in the morgue.

Valerie wondered if she would ever have to stand over the body of her younger sister and identify her. Would she ever be cured or stable? Would she be suicidal for the rest of her days? Would Valerie herself have the same fate...

"Valerie, are you okay?" Will said, softly bringing his friend back from her daze.

Valerie shook herself mentally. "Yes, I'm fine. Just thinking about the case."

Will stood and looked at her. She felt his stare. He clearly didn't believe her. He knew that something was eating away at her. Valerie could tell. But did he know how deep her trauma ran?

"Okay," said Will unconvincingly. "What's our next move?"

As if answering that question, the door to the mortuary opened. In stepped a young looking police officer, straight from the Academy. He walked nervously up to the agents and to Hank the coroner.

"I was told to ask for Agent Law?" the man said, his voice filled with nerves. Valerie knew he'd probably never dealt with an FBI agent before. Agents could have an air of authority about them. To the uninitiated, they could be intimidating.

Valerie tried to settle him down with a friendly smile.

"I'm Agent Law," she answered.

"They've managed to identify the victim. Her name is Daniela Mason," the officer blurted out.

Valerie considered the police officer for a moment. He looked like he had a thorn stuck in his mind.

"There's something else isn't there officer?" she asked. "What's wrong?"

"Well," he stuttered. "The girl's the daughter of a local judge. And the press found out she's dead from a leak. They are already hounding anyone coming in and out of the building for a scoop."

Valerie turned to Will. "Can you go and get Charlie?"

"Of course," Will answered. "What about the press?"

"Let them stew for a while," Valerie said grimly. "We can visit the victim's family. The killer showed remorse by closing her eyes after the murder. Maybe the family knows the murderer."

"Or," Will mused, his voice cold, "one of her family is the killer."

CHAPTER TEN

Valerie felt the man's hatred. It seeped out of his every pore. But he had good reason to hate. Someone had just brutally murdered his daughter.

"You've got to get this bastard," Tim Mason said, his eyes red and his teeth clenched.

The man's enraged face and body language were in stark opposition to the pastoral colors of the family room used for bereavements at St Clemens police station.

"We want to do everything we can," Valerie said. It was a phrase she had uttered to victims' families over and over again for years. But she meant it every time. She would do everything she could. To stop the killer from murdering again and to bring the families closure.

"Just get out there then and find him!" Tim Mason screamed. He then put his head into his hands and began sobbing.

Next to him, his wife, Janice Mason, cut a more sobering figure.

"Please excuse my husband," she said. "It is all quite a shock to us. We all loved Daniela."

Charlie and Will sat alongside Valerie. Charlie gave Valerie a knowing glance and then entered into the conversation himself.

"Janice," he said. "You're Daniela's stepmother right?"

"Yes," she said. "I didn't have the honor of being her biological mother."

Valerie knew this was a lie. If grief was pouring out of Tim Mason's being, it was deception that came from Janice. And where there was deception, Valerie always had to follow.

"Did you get on well?" Valerie asked.

"Eh…" Janice stumbled over her words and looked at her husband.

Tim looked up, wiping tears from his cheeks. "You know how it is with stepmothers and kids. It doesn't always work out."

"Was there ever any conflict between you and Daniela?" Will said, breaking his silence.

"Me?" asked Tim. "No... Why are you asking me these questions? Shouldn't you be out there looking for my daughter's killer?"

"They're just routine," Charlie offered.

"He means we're suspects," Janice sniped.

"Suspects?" Tim said with incredulity. "How could anyone think such a thing?"

"You're not suspects," Valerie said. "But more often than not, a victim knows the person who murdered them. It's our job to find out if that's the case here. Can you think of anyone who might have wished your daughter harm?"

"She was like anyone in their twenties," Tim replied. "She liked having fun. Most people liked her; sure she could be tough, but she'd had a tough life with her mother dying so young. She wouldn't put up with anyone's crap. I raised her well... We raised her well."

"So you don't think she had any enemies from her work, or from her dating life?" Charlie said.

"She didn't date. She'd been with her boyfriend Chris Malcolm for three years," Tim replied. "I didn't pry into that, though he always seemed like a nice guy. And Daniela would have hated me sticking my nose into her business. She was a grown woman. She kept private about a lot of her life."

Charlie took a note. "What about her friends?"

"She was really close to her best friend, Emily. They were like sisters."

"And what about her boyfriend?" Will asked. "Is he still on the scene?"

"I read her Facebook," Janice said. "She broke up with him a couple of weeks ago. It was quite the to-do, the way she went on about it. I was surprised she was dating him in the first place. I wouldn't have let my own daughter get involved with someone like that. But as Daniela always reminded me, I wasn't her real mother. Her boyfriend was a loser. He had a record."

"What sort of record?" asked Charlie.

Tim sighed. "Look, Chris is a nice guy. He had a record for fighting in a bar once. He got unlucky, punched a guy in the face during the fight. The guy tanks and hits his head on the ground. Chris would have been sent down for life if the guy hadn't woken up."

"He's not the type of person who should have been in Daniela's life. Or ours," Janice said sharply.

Valerie suspected that Janice was more worried about being associated with an ex-con than her stepdaughter's safety.

"I just can't believe anyone who knew our Daniela would have

39

killed her... Oh God..." Tim slammed his fist onto the table in front of him out of grief.

Valerie could see it was taking a toll on the man. But he had to tell them everything he knew.

"I need you to be as open with me as you can. Where did you last see your daughter?"

"We all saw her three weeks ago," Janice said, answering for her husband. "We all went out for dinner together. Us, Danielle and... Chris..." There was something in Janice's tone. She was resentful about that night for some reason.

"And...?" Valerie asked.

"What do you mean?" asked Tim.

"I get the sense that there was an issue. Perhaps after the dinner?"

"It's Chris, her boyfriend," Janice said snarkily. "He completely lost it over the smallest thing. I'm telling you, if you're questioning people, start with him!"

"He had a couple too many and got a little agitated with Janice when she pressed him about getting a job," Tim said. "I stuck up for Janice, then Chris had a go at me. But I know Chris, he wouldn't harm a fly. He was just drunk."

"Did he threaten anyone?" Charlie asked.

Tim sat in silence for a moment. "Yeah," he finally said. "Daniela tried to calm him down and then he got pretty angry at her. She was just trying to keep the peace."

"What did he say to Daniela?" asked Will.

"He said... He said..."

"He said," continued Janice, "that we didn't know what he was capable of. I took that as a threat. And I think he killed Daniela." Janice crossed her arms as though she had closed the case.

"I can't believe it..." Tim looked at his wife and then back at Valerie. "Maybe Janice is right. Maybe you should question Chris."

"We will," said Valerie. "But it will hurt the investigation if it's spread around that Chris is a suspect, so please don't accuse him of anything and don't speak with the press. It'll only muddy the water. Just because Chris got angry one night, it doesn't mean he's a killer. But we will look into it. We'll leave no stone unturned."

"Thank you..." Tim said, shaking Valerie's hand and then Will and Charlie's.

The three investigators left the room and walked down a corridor to the back of the St Clemens police station.

40

"Thoughts?" Valerie asked.

"I did get the feeling that Janice was being deceptive," Will offered. "But it could just have been that she initially wanted to hide that she and Daniela didn't get on."

"Yeah," said Charlie. "I'd be more worried about Janice making a stink in the newspapers than her being involved in Daniela's death."

"Still," Valerie said thoughtfully. "We shouldn't take our eyes off her just yet. But I tend to agree. Let's do some digging on the ex-boyfriend and bring him in for questioning."

"Can we still chase the Wendel Institute lead?" Will asked.

"I forgot about that," Valerie said. She instantly wished she had kept that thought to herself. She wasn't in the habit of forgetting.

She caught a look between Charlie and Will.

They think I'm not up to it. They think I shouldn't be here.

Charlie opened his mouth to say something.

"I'm fine, Charlie. I just didn't get a lot of sleep last night," Valerie said. As she said it, Daniela's dead face, a dead ringer for her sister Suzie, flashed before her mind's eye.

"I know you're fine," Charlie said. "But if you're ever not, you can tell us."

"We're here for you, Valerie," Will said. " I know I might not have known you as long as others. But the three of us have been to hell and back together in a short time. If you ever need to talk, I'm here."

Valerie sighed. "I went to see my mother." The words just came out of her mouth, as if they had sat there waiting to escape all along.

"How was she?" Will asked.

"I don't want to talk about it," she said, the pain was too great. "But please know I'm absolutely fine to be at work."

"And how does Tom feel about cutting your vacation short?" Will's questions were getting a little too close to the bone.

"It's fine. He's fine. We're fine. I'm fine. Can we drop it now?"

"Okay, okay," said Charlie. "But if you want to go back to your vacation at some point, I'm sure Jackson would…"

"No," Valerie said. "I just want to do the job. Now let's track down Daniela Mason's ex-boyfriend."

CHAPTER ELEVEN

The faces. The faces. They all looked the same to the killer. The same face he had to erase from the world. The same face that had injured him so badly.

Adrenaline was coursing through the man's veins. He could feel his heart thudding again and again inside of his chest. Paranoia bled through his mind. Were the people on the street watching him? Did they recognize him? Did they know what he had done?

It was mid-day and the sun was high in the sky. He could feel the sweat forming on his forehead. Beads of it ran down from his arms and down his back.

Slow down, he said to himself. *Slow. It's not all bad. They aren't looking at you. They don't care about you. You're just a passing stranger. Breathe.*

As the sun glared down, he walked passed some more people on the street, and then decided to head towards a quieter part of town. Less people. Fewer eyes staring.

Breathe. You are here. No one is watching you.

This was a trick he'd learned from one of the doctors during his treatment. He would center himself and remind himself that, although his paranoid state of mind might persuade him that people were looking at him, they were not. He was just another seed floating through the air of life.

People were too busy with themselves to notice.

I'm just a speck of dust.

Just as he started to feel more centered. It happened again. He saw that face. She was across the street from him getting out of a car. That face... A face he had to contend with for the rest of his life. It would haunt him until his deathbed.

Unless he could be rid of it. Unless he could finally wipe it out of existence for good. She would be the third one. It was getting easier to do it each time. He hoped it would be the last, but in his gut he knew. It was a face he would have to destroy again and again, until his soul was covered in its blood.

CHAPTER TWELVE

Charlie hated stakeouts. He hated all the waiting around. But sometimes it was necessary, and with few other leads to chase, he was hell bent on catching Daniela Mason's ex-boyfriend.

They had parked far enough away from Chris Malcolm's mother's house to remain unseen in the dark.

Will snored loudly in the backseat as the clock on the dashboard read 1:38AM.

Valerie leaned over from the passenger side. "Do you think he'd notice if we put him in the trunk?"

"He'd just persuade the trunk it had an existential crisis and it would let him out."

"I hope Daniela's ex turns up tonight," Valerie said sipping her coffee. "We're treading water right now. We've got to find a lead."

"Any luck with the Wendel Institute?" Charlie said, yawning.

"Not yet. We've been trying to contact the administrator. He's the only person who can grant legal access to the patient records. But he's on vacation somewhere in India. It's one of those retreats. No phone. No email. No electricity. Just five days out there drinking water and meditating."

"And no one else can give us those files to see who the released patients were?" Charlie asked.

Valerie shook her head. "Unfortunately not. The administrator has access to everything."

Will snored loudly again.

"I'm going to pinch his nose, I swear," Charlie said, looking over his shoulder at the doctor snoozing.

"You know you snore as well, right? Valerie said. "I think I'm the only one out of us who doesn't."

"I hate to tell you…" But Charlie's next quip was soon cut short. A car's headlights beamed brightly as they turned onto the street from behind.

Charlie and Valerie ducked down so as not to be seen. Charlie peered out over the edge of the driver's door.

A brown Kia. The same color and make as the car registered to Chris Malcolm. Charlie took one look at the plates and then down to his phone.

"It's him," he whispered to Valerie.

Once the car had passed, the two FBI agents sat up in their seats.

"We should wake Will," Valerie said in a low voice.

The car up ahead turned into the driveway of Chris Malcolm's mother's house.

Charlie watched as the car cut its lights and the driver's door opened.

Chris Malcolm stepped out of the car and Charlie could see the man's face in the moonlight. He was thin, with a round face and an almost comical expression. The man stretched, stood straight, and then waved to someone in the passenger seat.

"He's got a girl with him," Charlie said.

Valerie looked over at her partner. "So soon after Daniela's death?"

"It seems some people move on, quick."

Will snored again from the backseat.

"We should wake him up," Valerie suggested.

Charlie couldn't resist. He leaned over the seat and pinched Will's nose. Will opened his eyes with a gasp and sat up, holding his chest in fright.

"Very amusing," Will said, catching his breath. "You know, Charlie, I can easily forge a diagnosis and have you committed."

Will peered out from the backseat.

"Finally, he's here?"

"Yes," Valerie answered. "And he seems to have a woman with him."

"Well, we shouldn't read too much into that. She could be a friend," Will said.

The three investigators looked out as Chris Malcolm opened the door for the woman. She stood up, her blonde hair catching a ray of streetlight. They kissed.

"Or maybe we should jump to conclusions," Will concluded.

"Just because he's a scumbag," Charlie added. "Doesn't mean he's a killer. But it isn't a good look."

"Let's move," Valerie said stepping out of the car.

Charlie followed. "Chris Malcolm!" He yelled closing the car door. "FBI, we'd like to have a few words with you."

The man and woman froze and looked on in surprise.

"Oh…" The man stepped forward. "Daniela. Did you, um… Did you find her?"

"We found her," Charlie said. "And we found out a lot about you."

"Daniela?" The woman was clearly distressed, looking at Chris suspiciously.

Valerie took the lead. "Who are you?"

The woman's head shook in disbelief. "Chris's girlfriend."

"For how long?" Valerie asked walking off the street and onto the driveway.

"About two months," she said, still keeping her eyes on her boyfriend. "Who is Daniela?"

Chris didn't reply. He stood there, dumbfounded.

"Allow me to answer for him," Charlie said. "Daniela was Chris's girlfriend up until a couple of weeks ago. Someone murdered her."

"I know how this looks..." Chris said, holding his hands up. "But I swear I had nothing to do with that."

"You had another girlfriend?" the woman with blonde hair said, her voice wavering.

"The relationship was all but over when we met, Fran, I swear. I just didn't have the guts to end it sooner. But I did to be with you."

"That's beautiful," Charlie said sarcastically. "Now, would you mind telling us why you wouldn't answer our calls or the messages from Daniela's family these last two days? That looks pretty suspicious. All of this does."

Chris stood in silence.

"Aren't you going to answer him?" Fran asked.

But Chris didn't answer. Instead, he burst into a sprint and jumped over the fence into the next yard.

Charlie wasn't in the mood for Chris's antics, not after hours of staking out his mother's house. Charlie hurdled the fence and sprinted behind.

Chris was already panting. Charlie could hear him. The man was out of shape. Charlie was not.

Chris ran around the side of a house and then into another yard, but Charlie spotted a shortcut. He vaulted another fence. Then another. The darkness was Charlie's ally. His eyes were sharp, his ears even sharper.

He heard Chris panting, coming around a corner and entering the next yard.

Charlie climbed up onto the edge of a six foot high fence and then leapt onto his prey.

Chris screamed in fright. He reached out with his fist and tried to punch Charlie. But Charlie had the element of surprise. He pulled Chris to the ground in an armlock.

"If it looked bad before," Charlie said, out of breath. "It looks really bad for you now, Chris."

"I swear I didn't do anything!" the man screamed, his face buried into the grass.

Lights from around the neighborhood responded to the scream. Darkened windows glowed with curiosity and gossip.

Charlie pulled Chris up onto his feet. He marched him back onto the street where Valerie and Will waited with Chris's girlfriend Fran. She was sobbing.

"I didn't murder Daniela," Chris said to Valerie. "You have to believe me."

"Then why run?" Valerie asked.

Chris said nothing.

"Where were you the night she disappeared?" Valerie followed up.

Charlie held the man tightly in his grip so he wouldn't run again. Even if he had, he was too out of shape to outrun the agents again.

"Answer them!" Fran said, still sobbing.

But Chris hesitated.

Charlie looked over Valerie's shoulder and could tell Will was about to say something important. He had a way of turning his head slightly to the side whenever he was about to make an observation. Charlie enjoyed ribbing Will, but he was always amazed by his insight.

"Might I interject?" Will said stepping forward. "Going by your body language, Chris. I would say you're not worried about us finding out something. But you are angled away from Fran. It's poor Fran here who you're afraid might discover something. Perhaps... Ah yes... You were with another woman when Daniela disappeared weren't you?"

"Another one!" Fran said loudly.

Chris looked down at the ground defeated. "Yeah. I was away for a week with a woman from across town."

"You said you had found a job and you were working!" Fran said, her voice now angry.

"Sorry," was all Chris could say in his defense

"Can this woman verify your movements?" Valerie asked.

Chris nodded his head.

"Okay," said Charlie. "We'll check that. But even if you're not a murderer, Chris. You're still a scumbag."

Fran stormed off.

Valerie sighed. "Another dead end."

But fate intervened yet again to send the team in another direction. Her phone pinged. Valerie pulled it out of her pocket and read something.

"Yes! The administrator for the Wendel Institute just emailed me. He's flying back to the US tonight."

"That means we can get the list of released patients before the murders began," Will observed.

"Looks like our luck might just be about to improve," said Charlie. He knew they'd have to hold onto Chris until they could verify his alibi. But he felt it in his bones. Chris wasn't the killer.

But Charlie was glad the administrator was returning. Tomorrow would be another avenue. Another chance at catching the killer before he took any more lives.

CHAPTER THIRTEEN

It was 9PM the next evening and Valerie was feeling agitated. The administrator for the Wendel Institute had given them somewhat of a runaround. He had a canceled flight. Then he refused to give any access to the institute's records over the phone.

The FBI wouldn't get access unless he was there to meet them face-to-face.

Valerie knew that she could force a court order, but by the time it was given, the administrator would have finally been in the US. It was pointless.

And so, she, Charlie, and Will waited.

The sun had set.

They were currently waiting on the grounds of the Wendel Institute itself. It had been constructed in the 1970s. The main building sat on a large estate surrounded by fields and obscured by thick evergreen trees.

The grounds felt ominous in the dark. The shadows moved strangely as the branches of the evergreens swayed in a forceful wind.

The three investigators sat in Charlie's car, once again feeling like they were on another stakeout.

"No wonder they shut this place down," said Charlie.

"I have to agree," said Will. "The architecture is rather bleak authoritarian. Not conducive to a modern therapeutic environment."

Valerie stayed silent. Although she did not speak, her mind was a raging torrent of thoughts. The darkened windows of the Wendel Institute held stories for Valerie. Personal histories. Someone like her sister, someone like her mother, they were held in those rooms. Some treated successfully, others not so.

She did not know what the outcome would be for her own family. But those bleak blank windows were terrifying for Valerie. She felt as though she was destined to spend her days in such a place, if the same illness came for her.

"It's 9:15," Charlie said. "Did the administrator not say he'd be here at 8:45?"

"Yes," Valerie answered. "Considering how difficult it was to get

48

in touch with him, then the runaround he gave us, I wouldn't be surprised if he's significantly late."

Will leaned in from the rear seat. "Hold on, there's something that bothers me."

"Oh?" Valerie asked.

"Look over there to the east corner of the building," Will said pointing over Charlie's shoulder.

Valerie leaned forward slightly in the passenger seat. She scanned the rows and rows of windows, until she came to an unnerving sight.

There, hidden by the shadow of a large evergreen tree, was a window on the ground floor. All the rest were shuttered. All the rest were closed. This one was lying open like the maw of some terrible cave.

"It's the only window that opens," Valerie said out loud.

"I thought the whole building had been sealed since the Wendel Institute closed?" Charlie asked, setting up in his chair.

"Someone either forgot to close that window…" Valerie said trailing off.

"Someone is inside," Will said.

Valerie thought for a moment. The profile she had been considering for the killer did leave the door open for such behavior

"Let's say our killer isn't a complete psychopath," Valerie said. "We've witnessed a level of remorse and how he closed Daniela's eyes after killing her. If he has this emotional center, then he may be looking for…"

"A security blanket of sorts," Will said finishing her thought.

"He could be revisiting a place that he found safe. Looking for emotional solace," Charlie offered. "Especially a place like this. A place where he would have been given treatment during his worst episodes."

"He could be in there right now," Valerie said. Just as she did that a breeze whispered over the front of the car. The car shuddered slightly. The sound of the wind rustled in the trees. It sounded like a chorus of whispers. The voices of all the inmates and patients who had ever stayed, voluntarily or involuntarily, at the Wendel Institute.

Valerie thought she saw movement for a second in one of the windows. She couldn't be certain, the shadows played tricks. They always did.

"Did you see that?" Charlie asked.

Valerie drew her gun. "Let's move." She opened the glove

49

compartment and pulled out a small revolver and handed it over to Will.

Will wasn't an agent. But in a previous case he had been badly wounded by a serial killer while waiting alone in the car. None of them were willing to take that chance again. He would be armed, but he would stay back for now.

Valerie and Charlie left the car and headed towards the imposing institute building. A building that should have been empty, but someone was inside. And it may have been the killer.

They covered the ground as quickly and as quietly as possible. Valerie felt the change from concrete to grass and into concrete again. Each footfall brought with it a greater sense of urgency as the building and all its darkened windows neared.

Charlie pointed to the wide double doors. Valerie approached and gently touched the handles. It felt cold in the night. But there was no life to them; they were locked. She signaled to Charlie to keep moving.

Charlie moved along the side of the building. Valerie kept an eye out covering her partner. She watched with bated breath as he reached the open window on the ground floor. Now it was Valerie's turn. She moved quickly feeling the side of the building as she went. The wind caught her coat, making it flap slightly. The resulting sound blended in with the rustling of the tree branches all around.

She soon reached the back of her partner. Charlie was crouched, his back against the wall. Above him was the window. Valerie's pulse raced. The darkness inside the building seemed all-consuming. It was like a bleak well of nothingness.

Valerie brought herself closer to the window. She could feel the difference in there. It had a musty scent to it. She almost instinctively pulled out her flashlight to shine it inside. But she stopped herself momentarily.

Don't be silly, Valerie, she thought to herself. Shining a light like that in such a dark area would make her a sitting target to whoever waited inside.

Valerie knew that sometimes you had to take a chance doing fieldwork. And this was one of those times. She'd have to bet against the darkness. She steadied herself. She persuaded herself the killer wouldn't see her. If she were blinded by the darkness, then it wouldn't assist him either.

As quietly as possible, she reached up and gripped the window frame. She pulled herself up, and as she crossed the threshold into the building, the darkness swallowed her whole.

She strained to listen. It was the one sense she had to keep herself alive. To give warning against any coming attack. The building was settling all around her. It creaked and groaned occasionally. And in the not too far away rooms of the place, footsteps could be heard.

Charlie climbed stealthily up into the building. Valerie was always intrigued by his ability to be silent. He had told her much about his time in places like Iraq and Afghanistan as a soldier. Given his ability to move so quietly, she wondered sometimes if he'd been special forces, and if he were still bound to secrecy. Even friends have secrets from each other. She had some of her own.

There was absolutely no light. Valerie waited for a moment, until Charlie whispered next to her. "We're going to have to risk it, Val."

Valerie knew he was right, but despite all her years of experience, turning a light on in the darkest and most dangerous of places always still possessed a grim anxiety for her. She never knew what she would be confronted with.

Valerie put a hand in her pocket and pulled out her flashlight. With one arm outstretched, she flicked the light on. She half expected to see a maniacal grinning face just inches from her. But instead she simply saw chairs stacked up, some boxes too. It was a storage room, yet to be cleared since the Wendel Institute been shut down.

Valerie thought she heard something again. Those footsteps nearby. She knew Charlie's hearing was exceptional. She turned to him. In the dim light, he listened. And then he spoke.

"He's very close," he said. "I think he's coming this way. Get ready."

Valerie moved over to the nearest door. It was slightly ajar, the gap leading into the hallway filled with yet more darkness.

Yet this time there was something else there. There was someone moving around.

The footsteps quickened slightly, moving down the hallway with more purpose. Valerie felt a cold chill run through her blood. The footsteps were getting nearer.

They were heading directly to them.

Most killers fled from confrontation. They were creatures of self-preservation. This one, if he knew they were there, was emboldened by their presence. He was intent on confrontation. And it would be a violent one.

Valerie gripped her gun tightly. The footsteps moved, louder still.

51

Until, suddenly, they stopped. There was now only the doorway between the killer and the agents. But it felt like a chasm in the grim darkness of that place.

Suddenly, a man rushed through the door. Charlie reached out to grab him but was elbowed in the stomach, winding him.

"FBI! Freeze!" Valerie shouted. She reached out, grabbing the man by the wrist. He pulled back with force. He was large and quick.

His strength pulled Valerie forwards and she instinctively thrust the butt of her gun at the man. She caught him on the side of the head and he staggered back. But not for long. He moved forward again and lunged at Valerie. She darted quickly to the side, long enough for Charlie to stand up and wrap his arms around their assailant.

Valerie raised her gun and pointed it inches from the man's face. His eyes were wide in the dim light and he was panting heavily. He instinctively calmed as he stared down the barrel of the gun.

Valerie stared him down.

"Hands on your head and face the wall," she said, gasping for air.

Charlie pulled back to the side and the man did as she commanded, and Valerie then stepped forward, putting him in cuffs.

"Please, what do you want?" the man said, nervously.

"I'm Agent Law from the FBI," Valerie answered. "We're on a manhunt."

"And you might be that man," Charlie said, rubbing his side.

"What?" the man pleaded. "I swear, I just crashed here cause I heard the place was empty. I ain't done nothin'!"

"We'll see about that," Valerie said. "Why did you attack us?"

"I thought you were comin' in to steal my stuff!" he said. "Squattin' ain't easy. Soon as ya find a good place to crash, everyone wants a piece. If ya ain't willin' to fight for it, ya have to move on."

Valerie felt a pang in her gut. She worried he was telling the truth.

She glanced over at Charlie and he shook his head slightly.

At that moment, two bright headlights came into the grounds outside. They beamed through the night like two pokers of white heat.

"Now who's that?" the man in cuffs groaned.

"The administrator must finally be here," Valerie said. "Charlie, you check out this man's story. Will and I will speak with the administrator and see what he knows about the released patients."

"Come on," Charlie grunted, pulling the man by the arm and leading him out. "Let's see if your story checks out."

But Valerie already feared the answer to that, and it would put them back to square one.

    Unless, she thought, *the administrator has something to tell us.*

CHAPTER FOURTEEN

Valerie sat in the administrator's office feeling the cold of the Wendel Institute. It was as if the place emanated it. The room was brightly lit, but beyond it the vast labyrinthine world of the institute remained in darkness.

The administrator, a tall slender man in his thirties with a brown side parting and a keen gaze, sat behind a rich oak desk. On the other side, Valerie and Will sat on two uncomfortable plastic chairs.

Valerie's phone pinged with a notification. She looked down at it. It was from Charlie. He had taken the man they had arrested out of the building to run a background check on him.

The message read: *The man is a squatter, like he said. His name is Derek Ferguson and he broke into the building because it was empty. Not the killer. He freaked when he saw us. Apparently he was assaulted at a hostel a few weeks ago, that's why he was here. He got scared and attacked us. It's not him.*

Those last three words were a disappointment. But Valerie was getting used to the disappointment during this investigation. It was taking twists and turns, taking them around blind corners to unknown places, and each time they were being thwarted by fate.

"Agent Carlson has verified that the man we arrested wasn't a patient here, or the man we were looking for," Valerie said.

"That's a shame," Will replied. "I really hoped we had caught him this time."

"I doubt any old patients would have wanted to return here," the administrator said. "The treatments they used here, including an abuse of electric shock treatment, would be enough to give any legitimate psychiatrist nightmares. This was not a happy place for patients."

"It pains me to hear that," Will said. "I knew someone who worked at the institute, they were... They are respected."

The administrator leaned forward in his seat and placed his arms onto the desk. "Not everyone was a bad egg, Dr. Cooper. Perhaps your colleague was carrying out legitimate, ethical research. But there was enough mismanagement here and mistreatment of patients that they had to shut the place down and bring me in to oversee the transfer of patients and equipment to more ethical hospitals."

"How many patients were transferred to permanent facilities when the Wendel Institute closed?" Valerie asked.

"162," the administrator said, sighing.

"And how many were released back into the general population?"

"103," the administrator explained. "But they were mainly voluntary patients who, after strict evaluation, were deemed safe to continue their treatment at home."

"How many on the list were previously deemed high risk?" Will asked.

"There were 9 patients on the list who were highly violent in their early years before being successfully treated," the administrator said.

"That might help narrow things down," Will said to Valerie.

"If it's acceptable to you, Administrator," Valerie said. "I would really like to look at that list of released patients."

"I've been thinking about this," the administrator said. "But I still can't justify releasing that information to you at this time."

Valerie felt exhausted. She felt cheated. "Why did you ask us out here if you weren't going to show that information?"

"It was a courtesy to speak with you face-to-face, and I was uncertain when we spoke earlier on the phone," the administrator said. "I also had some other work I had to take care of here. Two birds with one stone and all that."

"Unbelievable," Valerie said under her breath. She looked up and saw Will's face. He had a concerned expression. Like he was surprised with Valerie's unprofessional response. She was surprised, too. *Maybe they're right*, she thought. *Maybe I should have finished that vacation and never got involved. My mind is all over the place. Keep it together, Val.*

"I think what Agent Law means to say," Will said in an apologetic tone. "Is that without your help, Administrator, another murder could happen at any time."

"I appreciate the fact that you're in a difficult circumstance," the administrator said. "But these are sensitive medical records. I can't so quickly betray doctor-patient privilege."

"But you're not a doctor, are you?" Will said.

"Well-put, Dr. Cooper," the administrator said. "But I do have a duty of care to the previous patients and their information stored here. At least until my duties as the administrator come to an end and this place gets bulldozed."

Valerie was racking her brains. She was trying to think of a way to persuade the administrator. She didn't want to have to go through a court order to get a warrant. It would take too long and there was no guarantee she'd get it. But her tired mind seemed empty for once. A tactical approach to such conversations normally came easily to Valerie. But not in that moment.

She was running on empty.

"What about *your* care of duty for the general public?" Will said.

"Again," the administrator said apologetically. "I understand where you're coming from, but I have a job to do and protecting the records here is one of them."

"I respect that," Will said tactfully. "I'm a doctor and I protect my patients' confidentiality. Priests protect the confidentiality of those who have confessed. But I can tell you, as a doctor, that when more harm will be done by protecting a patient's privacy, I have to choose the road of least harm. My duty isn't just to a patient but to others that patient could harm."

"If I had a patient who the police were looking for and they were suspected of being a violent murderer, I would have to assist."

The administrator paused for a moment. He seemed in deep thought. "Do you really think it could be someone from this institute?"

"I do," Will said. "And they are locked into a pattern of escalation. Two women are dead."

Valerie finally saw an opening. Sometimes people just needed a push to do the right thing.

She put her hand into her pocket and pulled out her cellphone. She pulled up a picture of one of the victims. Daniela's butchered body hung from the chain in the barn.

Valerie showed the picture to the administrator.

"Dear God…"

Valerie put the phone away.

"Do you have a daughter, Administrator?" Valerie asked, pointing to a framed picture that she'd noticed on the wall behind the administrator. It was a family photo of the administrator holding a baby dressed in pink.

"I do…" The administrator's voice sounded less sure, more anguished. The bloodied picture on Valerie's cellphone had provoked that.

"How would you feel if this is what happened to your daughter, or because of bureaucracy? That what could have saved her was a simple releasing of information to the people trying to track down a killer?"

The administrator shook his head with worry, rubbing his temples. There was a silence. A silence that seemed to echo through the empty rooms and halls of the institute.

It was oppressive.

The administrator finally nodded, glancing again at his family photo and back to the FBI agent and her colleague. "Here, take them."

The administrator handed over a brown paper envelope from his desk.

"Thank you very much for your assistance," Valerie said.

"I hope you catch the killer," the administrator offered.

"So do I," Valerie said. "But these names will help. You've done the right thing today. You might just have saved lives."

Valerie and Will left the room and walked through the darkened corridors of the Wendel Institute. When they reached the outside in the darkness, she found Charlie standing, waiting for them.

"Any luck?" Charlie asked.

Valerie handed the envelope to Charlie and said: "I know it's late, but let's get started. There are nine names out of the 103 on this list who were once violent. We can go check them out one by one. Hopefully we'll get lucky."

Charlie opened the envelope and held up a long list of names.

"There are a lot of others," he said, sighing. "What if our killer is one of the other 94?

"I know," Valerie replied. "But we have to start somewhere. We'll contact local law enforcement and see if Jackson can spare some other agents to interview the others. We'll focus on the nine."

She gazed at the list in Charlie's hand and wondered if the name of the brutal killer was staring back.

CHAPTER FIFTEEN

Michaela had always enjoyed jogging down that way. At one time the area had been home to a network of factories. Decades ago, they had been removed, and nature had slowly reclaimed the land.

It wasn't a public park, and few in the neighborhood would have thought about going there, but to Michaela it was a little island of solitude. A place to go to start her day in peace.

It was 6:30AM, and Michaela had been jogging through the neighborhood for about 15 minutes when she finally turned onto a thin trail that would take her through an abandoned piece of ground. Bushes and trees sporadically populated the surrounding environment, and there was no one else for company but for the occasional bird roosting in some of the trees.

Halfway along the trail, at her most isolated from the surrounding neighborhood, her daily routine was shattered.

Something was lying across the trail.

At first Michaela thought it was a pile of clothes that someone had just dumped there. But as she neared, she was able to make out the shape of a person.

Her heart began to race.

She stopped and stared. Birds were singing nearby, but they did not comfort her. Michaela had a growing dread now flowing through her blood. She looked back over her shoulder to the slip of trail she had already covered, as if hoping for someone else to arrive to help.

No one would. She knew that. It was her little place. She rarely saw anyone else out there, especially that early in the morning.

She wondered if the person on the ground was dead. It certainly looked like that, the way that they were spread out across the trail. No one in their right mind would have laid there like that out in the open.

"Hello?" Michaela said from about 20 feet away, hoping for a response.

At first the person lying on the ground didn't stir, but then she noticed a small movement. The person's right hand moved slightly against the ground. It was almost as if they writhed in pain.

Michaela implicitly assumed that they were hurt. Something was very wrong.

"Are you okay?" Michaela shouted. Her voice echoed between the trees and across the rest of the open waste ground.

She watched as the figure's fingers moved around in the dirt, almost clawing at it. It was a man... Definitely...

"Are you hurt?" Michaela asked, concerned now more than ever for the man's well-being.

But again the figure did not respond with words, but instead subtly moved on the ground as if unaware of her presence.

Michaela pulled out her phone.

She was worried for the man's safety. He was behaving as though he were badly injured. Nervously, she dialed 911.

The operator answered. "911, please state the nature of your emergency."

"I've found a man lying on a trail out at the back of Elm Street in Midway Town."

"Is he responsive?" the operator asked.

"I think so," Michaela said. "But he's lying on the ground like he's fallen or collapsed. He's moving slightly."

"Can you give us your exact address?"

"It's difficult," Michaela said, looking around at the large patch of waste ground populated by weeds, bushes, and young trees. "It's where the old gas works used to be, just behind Elm Street in Midway. They moved the factories years ago. There's no address"

"Okay," the operator said. "Please hold."

Michaela looked around at her environment again as she waited. She felt utterly alone. Helpless. She wanted to assist the man. But there was something inside of her telling her not to.

"Hi," the operator said, coming back onto the line. "I think we've got an address for where you are. I'm sending an ambulance; it's en route. Now, I'm going to need you to do something for me. Can you check that the man is breathing?"

Michaela's heart sank. That would mean getting closer to him. She had no desire to get too close, as fear was swelling inside of her. But she had to help him. She couldn't let him die.

"Well, he is moving slightly," she said. "But... It's difficult to tell from where I'm standing how badly hurt he is."

"Are you worried for your safety ma'am?"

"No," Michaela lied. She persuaded herself that her paranoia due to the isolation was taking over. "Should I do something?"

"If you feel safe," the operator said. "Approach him and see if he will respond to you. Ask him his name."

Michaela slowly walked towards the man lying on the ground. Her feet felt heavy from all the jogging she had been doing. But her heart was racing not just from that; it was racing because something deep inside of her was telling her to turn back. To go. To leave that place and the man on the trail. No good would come of it. Those words were like an omen in her mind.

But she did not turn back.

The warning in her heart was overridden by her desire to help.

"Hello?" she said as she approached.

She stopped just as she was standing over the figure.

His face was obscured by a jacket that had ridden up over his head.

The man's fingers on his right hand were moving. But his left hand remained obscured.

"What's your name?" she asked him, gently.

The man suddenly stirred, turned onto his back, and looked Michaela straight in the eye. She knew in that moment that she had made a terrible mistake. His eyes were wide and manic.

"You!" the man screamed as if he knew her. But he was a stranger to her.

His left hand now came out of his jacket pocket.

"Oh my God, he's got a knife!" Michaela shouted into the phone. "Help!"

The man reached up, grabbed the phone, and threw it into a bush.

Michaela had nothing else to do but run. There was no one else around to intervene. She turned, the knife ever present in her mind.

But her legs were tired.

Too tired to reach a decent speed, and the man's rapid footsteps were closing in.

"Please don't hurt me. I didn't mean..." But Michaela didn't get to finish shouting, persuading, pleading for her life. Instead, a terrible pain arched out of her back as a knife plunged through muscle and ligament into her left lung.

The air escaped through the hole.

She fell to the ground and saw the knife in the man's hand, now covered in her own blood.

She felt the blood in her throat and in her lungs. She was choking on it, drowning internally from it. Her hands reached up, weak, exhausted. The knife plunged down with force, and Michaela felt it sink deep into her throat as the man seethed through grated teeth.

CHAPTER SIXTEEN

Valerie was exhausted from staying up all night. But she had to; the list of 9 suspects had to be investigated at any cost, including sleep. The sun blinked over the horizon. Valerie stood in it for a moment. She closed her eyes and breathed in the morning air. She was tired. But she was on the hunt.

It was nearly 6AM by the time Valerie, Charlie, and Will got to the address. The first address on the list of released patients from the Wendel Institute.

As they left the car parked on a quiet street of Indianapolis, Will seemed nervous to Valerie. She didn't blame him. It had taken him some time to recover from the wounds of a previous case. He'd spent quite some time in the hospital. Now Valerie was asking him to come into the fray again.

"Should I wait in the car?" he asked.

"No, Will," Valerie replied. "We need your insights." And she knew that was true. She could feel in her bones that she wasn't on her A-game. She was flagging. Tired. Stressed. Worried about her family.

But that wouldn't stop her. Valerie had a killer to catch.

"It's this one over here," Charlie said, pointing to number 17, a small, terraced house.

They followed Charlie's directions and found themselves at the front door. Another door to another place. Another door that could equally lead to a catch or a dead end for Valerie. She feared the latter. It was only a matter of time before the killer murdered another woman.

Valerie knocked on the door. She expected the resident to come groggily out of bed. So she was surprised to see a man of Southeast Asian descent answer the door within seconds.

He was in his thirties. His hair jet black. He was tall and powerful. And he was wearing a training outfit.

"Hello," he said. "It's a little early for a delivery, isn't it?"

"We're not delivery people," Valerie said taking out her badge. "We're the FBI. Are you Tarron Saelim?"

"Yes, that's me," he said. He looked worried. If he was the killer,

Valerie was glad.

"What's this all about?"

"We're investigating two murders," Charlie volunteered. "And we have some questions for you."

Tarron's face went ashen. "I swear, that's all behind me."

Valerie glanced at Will. He gave a glance back. They were onto something.

"Can we come in?" Valerie asked, trying to be cordial.

Tarron nodded, letting the three investigators in.

Valerie looked around. The house was immaculate. It was definitely the house of a bachelor. Very few family photos. Nothing suggesting a partner. The house was minimalistic in its layout. White walls. A large picture of Sylvester Stallone. Another of Conor McGregor.

"You like combat sports, Mr. Saelim?" Charlie asked, pointing to the pictures as he sat down on a small leather couch. Will sat, too. But Valerie remained standing.

"I find them inspirational," Tarron replied. "Don't you? You look like you work out."

Charlie nodded.

Valerie was profiling Saelim. Clean. Almost to the point of obsessive. The house was pretty empty.

"You were released from the Wendel Institute recently, Mr. Saelim?" Valerie asked.

He nodded mournfully. "But I was there voluntarily. I'd served my time."

Valerie's ears pricked up. "And what were you there for?"

Tarron sat down. "When I was 18 I had a bipolar episode. I was convinced a friend of mine was transmitting ideas into my head."

"What sort of ideas?" asked Will.

"To do bad things," Tarron said, sighing.

"And what did you do about that?" Valerie asked.

"I attacked one night," Tarron said. "I was out of my mind. Put my best friend in the hospital, and I was committed to the Wendel Institute."

"How was your stay there?" Valerie took out her notebook and scribbled down a few thoughts.

"I heard rumors of some patients being mistreated," Tarron replied. "But the therapist I had there helped me. I was never put into Ward 17."

"Ward 17?" asked Charlie. "Was that where the mistreatment took place?"

"Everyone knew about it," said Tarron. "Some sort of experimental psychiatric treatment. Anyone who didn't respond to conventional treatments was sent there."

"But you weren't?" Valerie asked.

Tarron shook his head. "I got better and was free to go after a few years."

"But you kept going after that?" Will inquired.

"Sure," said Tarron. "Twice a week. I didn't stay there. But it was an anchor for me. Any time I felt the medications not working or the illness relapsing, I'd up the number of therapy sessions there."

"This Ward 17," asked Valerie. "Did you know anyone who went in there?"

"Sure," Tarron answered. "A few."

"Are you still in touch with them?"

"The institute frowned on staying in touch with each other outside. They said it could set our treatment back. So I never did. But while there, I saw what Ward 17 did to a few people. It wasn't pretty."

Valerie could feel Will tensing up. He took pride in his profession and its ability to help people.

"Are you aware of what the treatment protocols were in Ward 17?" Will asked.

Tarron laughed. "No, I was just a patient. But afterwards some of the guys were on pretty powerful meds. They were practically walking around like zombies."

"And after they came off those meds?" Will asked.

"Well," said Tarron. "Now you mention it, a few did become violent. But then they were violent before, so it was difficult to tell if the institute had made that worse or not. I can only speak for what Wendel Institute did for me, and it was a lot. A lot of good."

"So you have a history of violence yourself?" Valerie prodded.

Tarron looked uncomfortable to Valerie. He didn't like the conversation being brought back to that.

"Yeah, I did. But it was due to my condition. Now, look around you," he said pointing to his house. "If I keep my life clutter free, eat well, get exercise, and take my meds, I manage to stay pretty stable. When I hurt my friend, I wasn't responsible."

"May I ask," Valerie continued, "where were you on the 15th?"

"15th?" Tarron looked down at the ground deep in thought. He raised his head. "I was at work during the day, then the gym until about

64

10PM. After that, I came home."

"Anyone see you come home?" Charlie asked.

"Actually, yes," answered Tarron. "A buddy of mine ended up crashing here. He'd had a fall out with his girl."

"And he can confirm that?" Charlie continued.

"Of course," said Tarron, confidently.

Valerie was amazed at how together Tarron was after such a complete breakdown. She thought of Suzie and her mother.

Maybe there's hope for them. Maybe even me.

But then she spotted something. A woman's handbag hanging over a chair at the rear of the room.

"Do you have a girlfriend or wife, Mr. Saelim?"

"No," he said.

"A female roommate?"

"No, why do you ask?" he said.

Valerie noticed a change in his body language. His stance had changed slightly, leaning almost imperceptibly to one side. He was agitated. Valerie knew, she had struck a nerve. And when she did that, she knew to push.

"Since I've been here," Valerie observed. "I've noticed a few things. A woman's umbrella at the door. The scent of perfume. And over there, a jacket. Unless these are your things?"

"No," Tarron answered, sighing. "Look, I wasn't completely honest with you. I did attend the institute voluntarily, but…"

"You had a relapse?" Will interjected.

"Yes," Tarron said.

"Why did you lie to us?" asked Charlie.

"Because I know it looks bad. I did know why you were here. I got an email from the institute's administrator this morning."

Valerie was furious. The administrator had no doubt sent a mass email to all of the patients who had been released after the institute closed down. This gave them a heads up. If the killer received that email, he would have time to prepare for an interview, even skip town.

"Unbelievable," Charlie grimaced.

Tarron seemed to respond to this reaction. "He just said he felt we should know our details had been given to the FBI to help with an inquiry," he explained. "I think he felt he was duty bound."

"Duty my ass," Charlie said.

"You still lied to us, Mr. Saelim?" Valerie prodded. "Why?"

"Like I said," he explained. "I knew you were coming. I knew you'd see my violent record. And it would look bad if the institute thought I still required treatment when I was released."

"And what does this have to do with the woman's belongings around your house?" Valerie asked, getting back on point.

"Those are my sister's things," Tarron explained. "As part of my release, she signed a welfare order where she would spend a couple of nights a week here to make sure I was doing okay. But I really am doing okay. I've got my life back on track. I'd never hurt anyone."

Valerie considered him for a moment. He genuinely seemed stable, and he was committed to staying that way by taking his meds and seeking out therapy whenever he had a mental dip.

She felt sorry for him, having to explain his mental health and treatment to a bunch of investigators. To have to be accused of something he clearly didn't do.

"That's okay, Mr. Saelim," Valerie said. "We'll check your alibi. But, for what it's worth, I think you're doing great."

Valerie felt her colleagues bristle slightly. Charlie looked at her, concerned. But she saw so much of her sister and mother's struggles, even her own mental health struggles, in Mr. Saelim that she couldn't help but reassure him.

"Could you do us a favor, Mr. Saelim?" Will asked.

"Of course," Tarron offered.

"Do you think you could give us the names of everyone you can remember going into Ward 17's treatment program?" Will handed him a business card with Will's email address on it.

"Sure," Tarron said. "But some of them will just be first names. I'm not sure I can remember everyone's full names there. It was over a long period of time."

Will nodded. "We just appreciate your assistance."

"Could you give me your friend's details?" Charlie asked. "So we can verify your alibi? And the name of your gym?"

Tarron wrote the details down on a piece of paper and handed them over.

"If I can help with anything else..."

"Thank you," Valerie said. "We'll contact you if we need to. Please do get in touch with us if you think of anything else."

Valerie left the house first. Tarron had given her some hope. At least for her family, if not for herself. She breathed the early morning air, and for the first time tried to focus on positive thoughts. That, one day, her sister and mother would be as stable as Tarron.

"What now?" Charlie asked, yawning.

"One down, eight to go from the high risk names," Will pointed out.

Valerie rubbed her eyes. "We should get some rest when we can, but we've still got plenty of daylight today. Let's use it and check out the next name. Then we can head to a motel and sleep."

Will never said anything. But he looked deep in thought.

"Does anyone have a missed call from HQ?" he said, looking down at his phone. "I must not have had a good reception in there."

Valerie needed sleep. But she knew that wasn't going to happen. Peering down at her phone there were three missed calls and an urgent message.

She shook her head as she read it.

"We're going to need more coffee," Valerie said.

"Don't tell me..." Charlie grumbled.

"He's killed again," Valerie said. "We need to get over to the murder scene. Now."

CHAPTER SEVENTEEN

Valerie walked along the trail with Charlie and Will. It was a quiet place, somewhere that should have been peaceful, but she could already see the blood up ahead.

Police had taped off the area, and a few of them were trying to keep a handle on local news reporters looking for a scoop.

It had taken forty minutes to get to the small town of Midway, and by the time Valerie and her two partners got there, the word had already spread like wildfire through the surrounding areas.

A woman had been murdered.

Valerie was already aware of some of the details after speaking with a local detective at the scene by phone, en route.

"Agent Law, FBI," Valerie said, showing her ID to one of the police officers.

In return, the young officer lifted up some of the police tape, which Valerie, Charlie, and Will slipped underneath and beyond.

"Wait a second," the officer said nervously as Will passed. "Do you *all* have ID?"

Charlie showed his, but Will had nothing but an FBI visitor's pass to go in and out of the Mesmer building back at Quantico.

"I'm sorry, if you don't…" the officer said.

"He's with us," Charlie explained. "He's an expert in serial killers."

"Serial killers?" the officer repeated, sounding shocked. "My God, in Midway?"

"Keep that one under your hat."

They continued on towards the body.

"Sorry, Val," Charlie whispered. "I shouldn't have let that slip. We're not even sure if this is another victim from the same killer."

"It's okay," Valerie said. "We're all exhausted, Charlie. You're not going to be the first one out of us to make mistakes."

Will stopped and stared at the white sheet covering the body on the ground. It was soaked in blood.

"You okay, Will?" Valerie asked, concerned.

"Yes," he replied. "I still find it difficult to see scenes like this."

"You never really get used to it," Valerie said, gently patting him on the shoulder. "It'll be okay. We'll get the person who did this if we stick together."

"We should look at the woman's face," Will said, his voice filled with dread. Valerie sensed that he didn't want to look, but knew they had to.

Charlie leaned down, put on some latex gloves from his inside pocket, and then pulled the sheet back slowly, respectfully.

It was another woman in her late twenties or there abouts. There was a hole in her neck, and other stab wounds around the body.

"They look similar to the stab wounds we found on Daniela Mason's body," Valerie observed. "Like the killer was frenzied, in a state of panic or overcome with violent arousal."

"Don't you think she has a passing resemblance to the first two victims?" Will asked, looking at the dead woman's face, her eyes closed over.

Valerie certainly did feel that. The shape of the face. The color of the hair. She looked fairly similar.

Valerie crouched down to take a closer look at the body. "He stuck the knife in the throat. That could suggest not wanting to hear her speak? What do you think, Will?"

"I agree," Will answered. "There were wounds to the other women's throats as well."

"It could be," Charlie added, "that the woman represents someone who had authority over him. Like he's killing women who looked like her, but also removing their voices because they were instruments of authority. He wouldn't be the first killer to kill out of inadequacy."

"It's a good theory," Valerie said. "It can't be a coincidence that all three victims look similar. We're going to have to put this out there, that brunette women in their mid to late twenties should be extra careful until we catch this guy."

"*If* we catch this guy," Will said.

This surprised Valerie. He was normally so positive about cases.

"Why do you say that?" Charlie asked, taking the words right out of Valerie's mouth.

"Serial killers who pick their victims due to their appearance," Will said, "often go dark."

"That's true," Valerie agreed, thinking of high profile serial cases. "There are periods of activity then inactivity."

"Why is that?" asked Charlie.

"Because," Will continued, "you really can only kill the same person so many times before that urge is sated for a while."

"We may have a limited window of opportunity, then," Valerie suggested.

"So, he might kill one or two more times, then stop killing? For how long, Will?" Charlie seemed as concerned as Valerie felt.

"It's hard to say," Will explained. "But escalation usually takes place over a few weeks. We'd normally expect a serial killer to eventually make too many mistakes and get caught as the compulsion to kill overwhelms their ability to plan their actions. But this killer... He's not planning this. It's an urge at a base level. And eventually he'll get that urge out of his system, at least for a while. He could theoretically go years before he kills again after that, as the urge reasserts itself."

"Marlon Ivan in New York," Valerie said. "He went 56 years without getting caught for that reason. A few weeks of killing, then years going back to his wife and kids like nothing had happened. No evidence of any other pathological behavior His family maintained he was a loving father and husband. But the itch kept coming back. It was only once he was too old that he got caught. He tried to overpower a 20-year-old gymnast and she kicked his ass. That's how the police apprehended him and were able to link him to a bunch of cold cases."

"The idea that he could stay under the radar for years," Charlie observed. "That's terrifying. Time could be running out, then."

Valerie's pulse quickened. She felt ill through lack of sleep. But now, more than ever, speed was of the essence.

"We need to play this smart," she said. "There are too many people on the list from the Wendel Institute, and Jackson sent me a message that we'd have to wait a little for more agents to help cover them. We have to split up and check each name. Will, you can come with me; Charlie, you okay to fly solo?"

"Always," he said. "I'll check up with local law enforcement to see if any police departments recognize the names. I think that might be a good way to narrow it down."

"Agreed," Valerie said.

Valerie caught the eye of another police officer waiting nearby. He raised his hand.

"Hi," Valerie said to him. "You got something for me?"
"We've got a potential ID on the body," he said. "Michaela Strain, 28, lives here in Midway."

70

"How did you get the ID? She looks like she was out jogging by the way she's dressed. I'm assuming she didn't have any identification on her?"

"We knew her name was Michaela from the 911 call she made before she was killed," the officer explained. "Two of her friends were expecting to meet her before work. They've pretty much confirmed her identity, though we'll need a formal ID of the body. I thought you should know."

"Thank you," Valerie replied. "Has anyone contacted her next of kin?"

"Yes," the officer said. "One of the detectives is doing that right now. Do you want to meet with them?"

"One of our agents will do that," Valerie said.

"You don't think it's worth speaking with the family right now?" Will wondered out loud.

"No," Valerie said. "Look at this situation. Michaela is jogging up here, she happens to find a man lying on the trail. This isn't an ambush, it's a crime of opportunity. Again, our killer didn't think about killing, not until she tried to help him. We know this from the 911 call. She didn't recognize him or she would have said so. This isn't someone connected to her. She's only dead because she was in the wrong place at the wrong time and wanted to help."

"Punished for being a good person," Will said, shaking his head.

"Yes," Valerie continued. "She was. But it was more than that. It was being a good person and bad luck, possibly, for looking like the killer's other victims. My point is that the family won't know anything about this man because this man didn't even know *he* was going to kill Michaela. He didn't know she even existed. I doubt the family has any knowledge of the killer. But we can chase that up later; for now we'll let someone else do that interview. We've got all these names to get through in the meantime."

"You know, I've been thinking," Charlie said, thoughtfully. "Why was the killer lying down on the trail? Surely he wasn't just trying to sleep. There must have been something wrong with him."

"That's a good idea," Will agreed. "He could have been having some sort of psychotic event, one that was too much for him to handle in that moment. Poor Michaela came along at the wrong time."

She turned to Charlie. "Let's stay in touch, Charlie. You get started on some of these names; Will and I will check some others. And we'll liaise with the police here in Midway to see if there's anything worth chasing up with Michaela's family."

"With all due respect," the officer, who was still standing to the side, said. "I come from Midway. I think the least you can do for the victim's family is speak with them before you leave."

"I will speak with them, officer," Valerie said. "But the best thing I can do for them right now is bring Michaela's killer to justice. And that's what I intend on doing."

Valerie moved off with Will by her side. She understood the point, and she knew that cops from local areas were more attuned to people's feelings, but Valerie had to be economical with her time.

If their theory was correct, the killer could go dark at any point once his urges had been temporarily fulfilled. Then they would lose track of him. Time was of the essence, and so the team had to keep moving to uncover the killer among Wendel Institute's ex-patients. That meant heading out again with no sleep or rest.

Valerie thought for a moment about Tom and the vacation they had planned with his parents. Perhaps she would return there if the case was concluded in time. But she couldn't be sure. She wasn't sure of anything anymore. Not this case, and not her personal life. Not even her own mental health.

But all of that had to wait for the time being.

She and her team had to keep searching until they were too exhausted to carry on.

CHAPTER EIGHTEEN

Valerie gripped the steering wheel, the tension in her body fingering down her arms all the way to her hands. She was driving herself and Will to the next name on the Wendel Institute list.

The skies had opened up, the highway covered in rain. Glowing taillights beamed in front of her through the spray kicked up by the glistening wheels in the dim day. The swish of the water cascading down the windscreen meshed together into an unsettling white noise.

Will was in the passenger seat looking through his phone. He seemed to be intently invested in something. Valerie was happy with that. Her mind was a torrent of thoughts both personal and professional. Talking about it felt like opening up a wound or collapsing a dam that could never be put back.

The drive to the next suspect on their list would take about 40 minutes, Valerie was trying her best to think through the case, though her personal issues made themselves known intermittently. Intrusive thoughts that only increased her stress levels.

She wasn't in the mood for conversation. If she could have just kept driving through the rain until her life hit a streak of sunshine, she would have.

The indicator clicked on and off as she moved between the traffic, and the rain battled against the car roof overhead.

She thought of the thin metal ceiling between her and the elements. That was how she felt about her family's insanity. That there was a thin dividing line between her and her mother and sister in the psychiatric wards.

Then her thoughts turned momentarily to her father.

Where was he? Why hadn't the search through the FBI thrown up his whereabouts? There was something in the back of her mind about that which needled at her.

One thing more than any other worried Valerie as she drove towards the next suspect. In previous cases she had been able to push her familial worries to the side in order to maintain her professionalism. She had been able to think clearly about the killer she was chasing and their motivations. Only once she returned to the quiet of her apartment did those intrusive thoughts about her family make themselves truly know.

But not this time. Since reconnecting with Suzie and her mother, since trying to find her father, she couldn't go back to that serenity. She was in a storm and nothing could save her but to hold on for dear life and hope that it would pass.

She was so tired, and so exasperated, with unanswered questions that her frustrations were bleeding into the investigation.

The wiper blade scraped across the glass, letting out a slight squeak as it did. Each time, the road ahead became slightly more visible, only to then be reclaimed by the cascading rain from above.

Valerie turned inward again as its rhythmic back and forward almost hypnotized her.

She knew that her mother had important information for her about her family and her past. Retrieving that information was going to be difficult. She had held out hope that tracking down her father would help. But so far, even with the assistance of her boss Jackson and the FBI, her father was proving particularly difficult to find.

For a moment, Valerie's mind drifted so far into her family problems that she didn't see it before it was too late.

Up ahead on the road, through the sheets of rain, a red taillight moved erratically. First, it swerved right, then left. The taillight was attached to something huge and lumbering. Then a crack sounded, and an equally large black shape fell off the back of what Valerie now knew was a truck.

"Look out!" Will screamed.

Valerie only had the shortest of moments to respond to the object. It was a large piece of sheet metal, and it was hurtling towards the car.

Thrusting her foot onto the brake pedal, she felt the car lose control. The wheels slid in the rain as the sheet of metal, buffeted by the wind and rain, came ever closer.

She grabbed the wheel tighter and swung it to the side violently. The sheet metal scraped along the ground kicking up shards of concrete, flipped up, and then barely missed the driver's side.

The car swerved all over the road, and Valerie, her training kicking in, lifted her foot from the pedal and then pumped the brake. This allowed her to control the car more tightly, as it finally came to a juddering, screeching halt.

Valerie looked behind her to make sure everyone else on the road was safe.

Other cars had stopped and the sheet of metal was now lying motionless in the middle of the road. Thankfully, no one had been hurt. The truck up ahead pulled over and switched on its hazard lights. Valerie did the same.

"That was close," Will said, breathing heavily. "That was some driving, Valerie. You saved our lives."

But Valerie felt a great deal of shame. Deep down, she had only reacted because Will had shouted. She had been so wrapped up in her own problems, that she had almost driven straight into that piece of sheet metal. Both of them could have been killed.

I've got to wake myself out of this, Valerie thought to herself. *I can't keep losing myself in my own problems. Not while I'm on a case.*

"You okay, Valerie?" Will asked, tenderly.

"I'll be fine," she said. But she did not feel it.

There was a knock on the rain drenched window. Valerie lowered her window. Standing there in the soaking rain was the truck driver who'd swerved up ahead on the road.

"You okay?" the driver asked. "I saw that sheet metal nearly hit you in my mirror. This damn weather must have pulled loose one of the safety ropes."

"We'll be fine," Valerie said. "Doesn't look like anyone else was hurt. But we need to make sure that sheet metal is taken off the road."

Valerie got out and spoke with some of the other drivers, asking them to band together and help her pull the sheet metal off the road to the side. It was hard work, but she, Will, and the other drivers got it done. The driver of the truck said he would wait for assistance and make sure that the rest of the sheet metal on the back of his truck was secured.

Valerie and Will got back into the car. They were drenched from the rain. Cold and battered by the elements. Valerie looked at the time on the dashboard. It was still morning, and yet the day was as dim as the bleakest of nights.

"That was quite the experience," Will said, joking and soaked from head to toe. "Nothing quite like a brush with death to wake you up from your own exhaustion. A renewed appreciation for life is better than any coffee isn't it?"

Valerie rubbed her eyes for a moment, pulling the rain away from them. She didn't say anything. She kept playing what had happened over and over in her mind: That piece of sheet metal moving towards the car like a giant bat in the grim wind.

"Valerie, it's not like you to be shaken by such a thing," Will observed suddenly. "You're not yourself at the moment, are you?"

"I'm always myself. Who else should I be?"

"Normally you're an unflappable FBI agent, but recently you've been completely preoccupied in a way that I've never seen. I worry for you."

Valerie turned to Will. He looked rather comical, his hair a mess from the rain. His usual carefully crafted academic demeanor, swept away by the water and wind.

But despite his appearance, Valerie couldn't find anything comical about his words. She felt defensive. A need to protect herself even though she was not under attack.

"I'm getting sick and tired of you and Charlie questioning my mental state!" She let that statement sit for a moment before continuing. "I've opened up to both of you about what's going on. Yes, I'm having problems with my family at the moment. But that doesn't change my efficacy as an agent. I'm dedicated to the task ahead. I won't endanger myself, you, or the public. I don't want this mentioned again, do you understand?"

"That's your choice," Will said. "But maybe you should talk to Tom, if you can't talk to us."

"Tom is fine with everything," she said, knowing it was a lie. She thought about how things had ended on their vacation. He had been so disappointed, and who knew what his family now thought of her. First impressions were important, and she'd hardly made a stellar impact.

"And he was fine with you dropping your vacation to come here? You had told me all about the trip before you left. How it was so important to Tom. How you were nervous about it. Then you left his family home at the drop of a hat when it was such a big deal that you were finally there?" Will asked.

He had cut to the core of it. Sometimes she felt Will's psychological talents were so keen that they bordered on telepathic.

"Tom is fine. I'm fine. I'm asking you as my friend, can you drop this topic of conversation?"

"I trust you, Valerie," Will said. "But that doesn't mean I'm going to stop worrying about you."

Valerie started the car. It grumbled underneath a bed of rain.

"I can focus on the case, despite what's going on," Valerie said. "All I'm asking is that you and Charlie do the same. Don't focus on me or my state of mind. I'll take care of that myself."

"As you wish," Will said. "But you know I'm here if you change your mind or need to talk. About Tom, about the case… About your family."

"I know," she said quietly. "I'm sorry, Will. I just don't have it in me to go over it. But I do have the strength to catch this killer."

Valerie gently pushed the gas pedal and drove down the highway. The rain continued to fall in sheets, following them like a curse.

Valerie was perturbed by the conversation she'd just had with her friend. Being defensive every time people asked how she was doing was only going to lead to conflict. If Jackson had seen how she had been acting, he'd have had serious issues with putting her back in the field.

She tried to take some of her own advice.

She had to focus purely on the case. Not on her family. That meant sticking to the road ahead, through the rain, through the gray, not stopping until they were face-to-face with the next suspect on the list.

CHAPTER NINETEEN

Valerie didn't like the look of the apartment building in front of them. It looked like most of it was empty, the windows covered up with sheet metal. She noted that it looked like the same metal that had fallen off the truck and rushed towards them in the rain.

Inside, she felt that was an omen.

The building was a square block of apartments, the gray long since covered in thick blankets of damp mold.

"Someone actually lives here?" Will asked almost rhetorically.

"People live in all sorts of places," Valerie said. In the back of her mind she wondered where her own father lived, if she could ever track him down. Was he, too, hiding in some run down place where people feared to tread?

She shook that thought.

This was about the case, not her.

Valerie looked down at the name on the piece of paper in her hand. "Owen Edgerton," she said. "That's who lives here."

"Any information about his time at the Wendel Institute?" Will asked.

"No, not yet. I'm still waiting on the background checks from HQ. Charlie has contacted local PDs as well."

She looked at the place in front of her. It looked so damp, she could almost taste it. The building was five stories high, and it looked like it had been thrown up during the 1970s. It was once new and filled with possibilities, but now it had succumbed to neglect and age.

The neighborhood was pretty empty as far as Valerie could see. It was a bit of a ghost town, sitting just south of Indianapolis, far enough away from the metropolis to have an isolation of sorts. It was one of those outskirt projects where developers tried to turn an almost rural area into an up and coming market for young professional couples.

It hadn't worked. Now it was being used by people who couldn't afford to go anywhere else. Valerie hated thinking of that. Everyone deserved not just a home, but a place that was safe and clean in which to rest. Whoever still lived inside that apartment had not been given the dignity of that.

"Let's go in," Valerie said putting the piece of paper back in her pocket. "Keep your eyes open, Will."

As they wandered through the front door of the apartment building, Valerie could feel Will tensing up. For all his many months of experience working at the unit, and his countless years of academic study into the minds of violent killers, he was still green enough to be affected by an insidious apprehension.

The shadows were more fearful to him than they were for Valerie. But even she had an oppressive intuition about that building, and it put her on edge.

The inside of the building smelled as damp as she had imagined. There was a sound of dripping water somewhere, but the water itself remained unseen. Valerie imagined that it was pouring into the building from a hole in the roof, but it could just have easily come from a broken pipe that no one wanted to mend.

The central stairwell had only one working light on the ceiling; the others had been smashed, and the shattered glass intermingled with litter on the concrete steps, so that their footsteps crunched like in frozen snow.

"I can't believe someone would live like this," Will mused in whisper.

"Some people are forced into it," Valerie answered. "People not being able to afford rent, landlords putting them into decrepit buildings. And often the tenants have little to no social support. It's an all too familiar story. I've seen it time and time again. But that doesn't mean we should let our guards down."

They moved up the stairwell to the next floor. Valerie pointed to a dim doorway. Will followed silently, his eyes darting to the shadows. His nervousness was almost contagious. Valerie could feel the apprehension in the damp air, and on more than one occasion she glanced at Will, only to see that he was paler in the dim light than usual.

The quiet dripping sound from somewhere in the building was now joined by another more bone chilling noise: the sound of a human voice mumbling in the darkness.

It meandered along the hallway, reaching out from the shadowy recesses of that place to Valerie and Will, bathing them in a shiver of uncertainty.

"Where is that coming from?" Will said in a nervous, whispered voice. It was as if he didn't want to be overhead by the voice in the darkness.

Valerie thought the worst thing the voice could do would be to utter either of their names.

Calm those thoughts, she commanded internally. She knew paranoia could quickly take hold of a person, and she wondered if thinking about voices speaking your name was how Suzie first became ill in her teens.

Valerie moved her hand to her side instinctively. It brushed against her holstered revolver. She was just checking it was there. It was a habit that she had when entering into more dangerous territory. Just feeling it there made her somehow feel safer. Like she could take action when needed; she couldn't be certain that the darkness wouldn't consume her, but she at least knew she could put up a good fight.

But there was never a guarantee of how such a confrontation would turn out.

Valerie's steps sounded against the hard concrete floor. If there ever had been the soft cushion of carpet or the polished sheen of wooden flooring in that place, it was long since gone. Rotten away or torn up by time.

Moving slowly, Valerie saw a light coming from an open doorway. She looked at the number on the door, which was hanging by its hinges in the bleak long shadows cast by the solitary light inside. A horrible stench came from inside.

"This is the one," she whispered to Will.

The voice continued to mumble from somewhere nearby.

Reaching out with her left hand, she knocked on the open door and finally spoke in a commanding voice. "Owen Edgerton? This is the FBI. We're wondering if you could answer a few questions?"

A few mumbled words came from inside the apartment. Now she knew for certain that was the source. The light in the apartment hallway suddenly switched off. Valerie stepped back, ushering Will to the side to safety.

"Owen," Valerie said calmly. "I want you to know that I *am* armed. I want you to know that, in case things get out of hand. If you answer me, and then speak with us, you can go on about your day without further incident."

Will looked at Valerie nervously.

She tried to give him some reassurance with a glance and a nod as if everything was okay. But in Valerie's line of work she had gotten used to knowing when things were going to go bad. She could feel it in the air like a bleak sky before a lightning strike.

Something was going to happen. But she had no idea what. She could feel her blood pressure rising in anticipation.

"Owen?" she said once more. But the darkness only mumbled words in response.

She couldn't quite make out what those words were saying. She strained her ears to make sense of the garbled words, but they melded into each other. She wished Charlie had been there with his keen hearing. That was always a handy talent to fall back on when going into the world's darker places. If one couldn't rely upon their eyes, then their ears would have to do.

She waited again, but the mumbling only became more fervent. At this rate, she was going to have to step inside.

Thankfully, Will interjected to try his own tact.

"Owen," Will said with surprising calm. "We're not here to hurt you. I'm actually a doctor and psychologist; I'm not an FBI agent. We're not accusing you of anything. We only want to have a quick chat about your time at the Wendel Institute. It might help us solve a case."

It was then as if the darkness gasped in response to Will's statement, to the mere mention of the psychiatric hospital. This was followed quickly and sharply by an inhalation of breath and then one particular word.

Valerie definitely made sense of it this time. It was definitive.

The voice whispered: "Wendel."

But that word sounded closer than the previous mumbling to Valerie. And that intuition was correct.

Moving at searing speed out of the darkness, something lunged at her, white arms and fingers flailing and grabbing at her like tentacles before her eyes. A stench of dirt and human waste came with them.

The fingers and hands groped at her face.

She tried to fire her gun, but it was too late. The thing from the darkness rushed forward, knocking Valarie's gun and hand upwards as it fired. The bullet splintered in the doorway above. Following immediately was a white, topless, emaciated figure, all skin and bones, but still strong and fast.

The man lurched further forward and smashed his jagged shoulder into Valerie's stomach, battering her to the side. Her body slammed into the doorframe, and she knocked her cheek into the solid wood. The impact shattered up her body, knocking the wind out of her lungs. She felt as though one of her ribs cracked with the force.

Momentarily dazed and helpless, Will reached out and grabbed the emaciated figure. But despite its thin, gaunt appearance, the attacker was able to quickly break Will's hold, pushing him back away from the doorway.

Valerie looked up to see Will try vainly to fight the man, but the attacker had the upper hand. His reach was better than Will's.

The man's wild, long, matted hair moved around as if blown by a gust of wind, revealing devilish eyes and a gaze hellbent on murder, hellbent on pain.

Will managed to punch him on the chin, but the man was in survival mode. He would not relent. He opened his mouth, obscured mostly by a beard smeared in dirt, and screamed.

The man reached out with blistering speed, retaliating and striking Will on the face. Will let out a gasp of air and fell to the side onto the floor.

The attacker looked around as if looking for his next victim.

In that brief second, Valerie felt he was weighing up whether to finish them off or not. He instead opted to flee the scene. He started to move down the hall. Will stuck out his foot and managed to trip the man by catching his ankle.

The man stumbled, but it wasn't enough. He found his footing and kept going down the hallway, mumbling something garbled and threatening.

Valerie scrambled up onto her feet.

Will was too dazed to move as quickly as she needed him to, so he waved his hand, intimating that he was okay and that she should get after their attacker.

Pushing past the pain, Valerie was now standing tall. Her side ached, but she was breathing better. Rushing ahead, she was afraid that she was about to lose the killer once again as he moved further away around a corner. With all her determination, she steadied herself, took a deep breath and chased after the man.

Valerie heard Will somewhere behind, clambering to his feet and following as best he could. Both of them rushed forward one after the other into the bleak darkness of the building, giving chase and hoping beyond hope that things would not get worse.

It was a flight into the unknown, and the killer could have been around any corner. But duty called, and Valerie wouldn't give up so easily.

CHAPTER TWENTY

Officer Mitchell handed the Styrofoam cup to Charlie. The coffee was hot. But it was warmer than the room at the old police station. The room was bathing in a buzzing, failing fluorescent light. The walls were a cold white, and the paint covering them had cracked in several places.

The police station was located in the town of Thornlake, near Indianapolis. It had seen better days, and so had the grizzled figure of Officer Mitchell, who sat across a creaking wooden desk from Charlie.

Charlie felt the Styrofoam cup in his hand, a relic from the past.

"I thought they didn't make these things anymore?" he said, pointing to the cup. He knew they were bad for the environment, but he didn't want to irk the elder police officer, not when he was there to find out information. He needed to know about the patients on the Wendel Institute list of those released after its closure.

Thirty minutes after sending a request to local police departments in the area with the names, Charlie received a call from Officer Mitchell, and so he'd headed over there right away, still exhausted, but he felt he had at least another few hours in him before he would absolutely require rest.

Officer Mitchell looked at his own Styrofoam cup and took a swig. The way he drank it, Charlie wondered if there was something more than coffee in there.

Mitchell eyed Charlie and then said gruffly: "They don't make a lot of things these days. They bring in new things, but they're rarely better." The officer smirked.

"If I listened to all of the advice people put out here these days," he continued. "I'd be better in the grave: I shouldn't drink off duty. I shouldn't eat steak. I shouldn't get so damned angry at my job. But, I keep doing all that. Life's for living. You learn that when you see so many people cut down at a moment's notice."

Charlie nodded in partial agreement.

A phone sitting on the officer's desk rang abruptly.

He answered it without even apologizing, "Mitchell." He announced to the caller. "Uh huh. God dammit. Let me look." He started rummaging around some drawers in his desk, pulling out files and pieces of paper that Charlie was certain were part of a unique filing system.

He'd known guys like Officer Mitchell back in the army. They were hedonistic. Work hard, play hard.

Whenever their tour came to an end or they got a break from where their camp was stationed, they'd head out and live life to excess.

Charlie didn't agree with it, necessarily. It was a reckless way to be, but sometimes he admired that sense of abandonment. He wouldn't have minded cutting loose now and then when things got tough. Just to blow off some steam.

But Charlie had chosen his life. He was a father of two, a husband and a partner. He had responsibilities he would never sacrifice for a quick thrill. It was his commitment to those around him that had seen him through some of life's hardest moments.

He took a deep drink of the coffee and tried to wake up as Officer Mitchell looked at some notes from his desk.

"Yeah, got it," Mitchell finally said into the phone. "Well, I don't know! Have Gill do it. He likes this sort of thing. I'll take a looksee later. Yeah, yeah. Bye."

He hung up and took another drink of coffee.

Charlie followed suit.

The cheap coffee machine had burned the coffee to a crisp. But it would have to do. Charlie needed something to keep himself going, and he wasn't about to do anything else.

He tried not to grimace as he cut to the point.

"Officer Mitchell," he said.

"Call me Mitchell," the old cop said. "Everyone else around here does."

"Mitchell, those names I sent to you…"

"Yeah," he sighed. "I looked at that list you gave us. Most of those names don't mean anything to me."

"But some do?" Charlie said, interjecting hopefully.

"One name…" he hesitated. "One name did stand out bright. That's Jason Richardson. He did some pretty sick things around here twenty years or so ago."

"I was the one that put him away. I was pretty happy with that, until they deemed him mentally ill, whatever that means. He got sent to the Wendel Institute. I hear they were a bit rough on some of the patients. Couldn't have happened to a nicer person."

Charlie again didn't argue the point. Catching the killer was more important than reminding Officer Mitchell that places like the Wendel Institute had a duty of care to patients, especially those who were the most challenging.

"What can you tell me about Jason Richardson?"

It was as if he didn't hear Charlie. He was too busy venting.

"First they don't send him to a proper prison, then you tell me the Wendel Institute has shut down and they've released him and a hundred more like him onto the streets?"

"Most of the patients are probably well adjusted," Charlie said. "But we were hoping to find someone on the list who would have the behavioral characteristics to murder once out. That way, we'd have a lead to stop a killer in the area."

"This type of thing really grinds my gears. Letting just anyone roam the streets. And after the stuff he pulled." The old cop poured another cup of coffee, took a long swig, and then shook his head as if disagreeing with someone in the room.

"This guy Jason," Charlie asked, trying to keep him on track. "What sort of things was he into?"

"Torturing animals," Officer Mitchell said. "He was sick. Did all kinds of things, but you won't find most of them on his record. It's only the stuff local cops would know."

"The crimes you couldn't quite prove?"

"Not enough to arrest him, but me and boys at the precinct knew he was responsible for a ton of perverted stuff he never got time for."

"And what did he finally get arrested for?"

"He threw his next door neighbor's poodle into a cement mixer."

Charlie grimaced inside. Something he could never understand was cruelty to animals. After all the horrors of war he had seen, he could sometimes understand how an unstable person might want to punish human beings, but not dogs and cats.

But this was something he continually encountered in his job with Val. Charlie knew that killers, especially serial killers, often started exploring torture and murder by killing animals first, then later moving on to humans.

"And that's what got him put away?" Charlie asked.

"No, not exactly," Officer Mitchell said. "It was what he did to Julie Memphis that put him under the nose of the shrinks. Julie was a local girl in Thornlake, a couple years younger than Jason Richardson. He had real sway over her. Really got under her skin like psychos can do.

Manipulated her into doing all kind of things. She was only 17. Before that, she was just a kid that got up to mischief sometimes. Usual teenager stuff, you know?"

Something buzzed loudly above their heads. It was the light fitting.

"Dammit," Mitchell said. He stood up, reached up high and smacked the side of the light to make it stop. Then he sat back down and took another slurp from his cup.

"Everything's falling apart around here," he laughed. "Including me." He scratched his chin as if lost for a moment. "Where was I?"

"Julie Memphis," Charlie offered, feeling that the burned coffee hadn't quite woken his mind up.

"Yeah," Officer Mitchell said. "She got her hands on some Xanax. For the two of them to party with. Anyways, an argument broke out between them while they were on it as far as we could tell. She'd had enough of his darker side, I think.

"Jason didn't take kindly to that. He beat the poor girl so badly she was in a hospital for two weeks. She was eating food through a straw because she had to have her jaw wired shut. I swear, if I could have had some time alone with him…"

"So, that's when he was arrested."

"Second charge after the dog incident. Me and my partner Don, he's sadly passed on, we got to put Jason Richardson away." He sighed, gritting his teeth momentarily.

"That's when the psychiatrist got involved. This academic know-nothing about the world came in. He interviewed Jason and the courts sent him to Wendel Institute. I hoped he'd spend the rest of his days there. That kid is pure evil."

"Do you think he could be a serial killer in the making?" Charlie asked, almost hopeful that he'd identified someone who fit the crimes.

"Definitely," Mitchell said, not hesitating for a moment. "You know, I've never forgotten the mess he made of Julie Memphis's face. When I saw that name on your list, I had to contact you. If someone's been doing something terrible, and that Jason was around in the vicinity, he's either involved or an accessory. I'd just straight up assume that."

"I really appreciate the heads up," Charlie said, though he wouldn't be assuming guilt until he had something more concrete.

He stood up and shook the old cop's hand.

"You know, my boss at the bureau's pride is going to be hurt," Charlie smiled. "You were able to snag that name on the list before the

FBI's database was able to."

Officer Mitchell smiled back, showing a lighter side. "Sometimes you just got to ask a beat cop if you want to know what's really going on in a neighborhood. I just wished I could tell you where this scumbag is now. He'll avoid this town like the plague because of cops like me, but I reckon he'll be in one of the surrounding places. A lot of small towns out here for slime to hide."

Charlie left the office and smiled to himself about his encounter. Officer Mitchell came from a time when officers overstepped the bounds on the regular. They were rougher around the edges. But he had the real feeling that, when it came down to it, Mitchell would have stuck to procedure and doing what's right more than he let on.

Outside, a ray of sun broke through the blanket of clouds above. As Charlie walked to his car and moved his tired joints, he felt hopeful for the first time in days. The team had a killer to catch. So far, they had been going from one dead end to another. But now there was a real possibility on the bleak horizon.

Jason Richardson was now suspect number one. All Charlie had to do was find him.

CHAPTER TWENTY ONE

Charlie looked at the bar on the corner of Main Street in Winslow Town. Another small, quiet place for a killer to hide in plain sight.

It had taken Charlie only a couple of hours to locate Jason Richardson. He'd taken Officer Mitchell's observation to heart. He inquired with several other police departments in the surrounding area, and finally one had given him several locations to check out.

After being told that Jason Richardson had a girlfriend he'd been in touch with while at the Wendel Institute, Charlie paid her a visit. She in turn told Charlie she didn't want anything to do with the man. Apparently he was far creepier out of the institute than he had been during day visits and in his letters.

The ex-girlfriend gave Charlie the address where he was staying: 106 Main Street, Winslow Town.

And so there he was. Waiting outside the bar, thinking about whether to stake the place out or go in. On his own. But that was okay. He loved being part of a team, but working solo helped keep his senses honed.

Looking out of his car windscreen, Charlie was slightly perturbed by what he saw. He thought he was going to an apartment block. But what he didn't expect to find, was that the given address was a small apartment sitting above a local bar. In fact, it was part of the bar, and the owner was letting Jason Richardson live there until he found another place.

Why that was, Charlie didn't know. But given the terrible stories he'd now heard about Jason Richardson from several police officers, the owner was either being pressured, involved in something nefarious, or just plain naive.

The bar was called The Bulldog. It was British themed, complete with a poorly painted caricature of Winston Churchill above the door.

It looked pretty rough. But that didn't matter to Charlie. He'd been to far rougher places. To the deserts of the world. To the most war torn places in existence. He could handle a few drinkers who might be a little too keen for a fight.

Stepping out of the car, Charlie felt he'd been waiting long enough. It was time to go in. It was time to bring Jason Richardson in for questioning.

He crossed the street and walked past two patrons of the bar who were arguing about who should buy the next round. They were both red faced and clearly worse for wear. There was a lot of pushing and swearing. But Charlie wasn't about to get involved. He had bigger fish to fry.

Walking through the door, Charlie was struck by the smell of the place. The bar immediately reeked of stale beer, and Charlie looked at the beer soaked wooden floors and stools around him, wondering if they even cleaned the tables in a place like that.

There was a Union Jack behind the bar, and most of the draft beer was from the UK. Behind the bar, wearing a shirt rolled up to his elbows and giant sideburns which wouldn't have looked out of place back in the '70s, the barman grinned widely as Charlie approached. He was short, his face as red as the handful of drinkers in the room. Charlie instantly felt that he was drinking on the job. But it was probably a professional hazard.

The way he carried himself, Charlie implicitly felt that he was the owner of the bar.

He could feel the looks of suspicion from the people around him as he stopped in front of the man. This was the type of place that hardly ever had new customers. It was all regulars, the type who would wait outside in the morning for the place to open, so that they could drink away what little money they had on them.

He felt sorry for anyone caught in such an addictive cycle.

"What can I get you?" the man behind the bar said in a thick British accent. Charlie was pretty sure the accent was from the North of England. Probably somewhere in or near Manchester. He'd served alongside a number of English soldiers, who called themselves "squaddies" in Iraq, and one in particular was from a town near there.

"That accent, you're not from Stockport are you?" Charlie said, thinking of the soldier he'd served with.

The barman grinned. "Ha! No! Macclesfield. But not too far from there."

"Are you drinking today, lad?"

"Another time, maybe."

"Then what can I do for you?" the barman said. His grin was still there, but Charlie noticed a change in his eyes. He wasn't pleased that

Charlie was there.

"I'm looking to have a chat with someone," Charlie said. "I believe he's currently staying upstairs."

"I wouldn't know about that," the barman said. Charlie could tell he was lying.

"Oh, really?" Charlie pressed. "Aren't you the owner? And shouldn't the owner of a premises know who's living in one of their rooms?"

The barman leaned into the bar. "I wouldn't know."

Charlie noticed that he suddenly seemed nervous. *He's afraid of Jason Richardson,* Charlie thought.

Pulling out his wallet, Charlie revealed his ID. "I'm FBI. I'd like to speak with Jason Richardson."

The man scratched his chin. His faced flushed even redder than before. "I... I thought you were law. I could tell. But I *can't* help you."

"Are you sure about that?"

The barman nodded unconvincingly.

"Anyone else know a Jason Richardson?" Charlie asked loudly, looking around.

Several of the people there looked down at their glasses as if Charlie didn't exist. But he knew they were just evading him.

One man caught his eye. A tall man with a ponytail and a blank expression. He was staring at Charlie and wouldn't look away.

Charlie turned back to the barman and looked around the place at the unsanitary conditions. "I wonder if a health and safety check would be in good order in this place? Unless of course, you can help me."

The bar man waited for a moment as though he were mulling it over.

"I don't know who you're looking for," he said. But this time, he moved his eyes to the side and tilted his head in the direction of the man with the ponytail.

Charlie whispered. "Thank you."

He turned to look at the man.

"Hello, Jason," he said, staring at him.

The man stood up, tall and gazelle-like. He hurdled over a table and headed straight for the door trying to make his escape.

Anticipating this, Charlie rushed towards the doorway to cut him off. As they both reached the exit at the same time, the man immediately switched from flight to fight.

The man reached out and struck at Charlie. Charlie bobbed and weaved, dodging the first strike. But Jason, and Charlie was certain that was who he was, obviously had some boxing training before. He countered with a left jab and caught Charlie as he ducked, square on the nose.

Charlie felt his nose bleed. But there was little pain. There was too much adrenaline coursing through his veins for that. But the problem was that his eyes welled up with water in response to the impact on his nose.

For a moment, he couldn't see.

Charlie knew he had to protect himself until his eyes cleared. He instinctively tucked his head down slightly and raised his hands up to guard his face from further attacks.

And those attacks did come.

Jason let go a torrent of explosive blows to Charlie's head and body. Charlie's guard caught most of them, but a few made it through, knocking him backwards.

He felt dazed and knew he wouldn't withstand a second barrage without being able to see, so he created a diversion. He sidestepped, felt for a glass from a table next to him, grabbed it, and then smashed it on the wall next to Jason.

The glass shattered, raining them both with shards.

Jason was taken by surprise enough for Charlie's moment to come. His eyes cleared, and now it was his turn to attack.

Charlie assessed his opponent and saw an opening. Jason was clearly trained in boxing, but he'd shown no skills in grappling.

Charlie stepped forward, grabbed Jason Richardson's sweater at the chest, pivoted his hips and tossed the man over his shoulders, slamming him onto the ground.

Jason gasped like he couldn't breathe from the impact. He tried to get up, but Charlie was on top of him quickly. He thrust his knee into Jason's back, pushing him onto his front, smacking his face into the floor.

He was done. All he could do was whimper and groan after that. Charlie didn't take enjoyment in violence, even though he was good at it. But for once, he allowed himself some satisfaction, given the man's history with killing animals.

Reaching into his pocket, Charlie produced two cable ties and wrapped them around Jason's wrists.

"I'm innocent," Jason groaned.

"You don't even know what the charges are, yet," Charlie said, catching his breath.

"I swear, whatever it is, I didn't do it."

"Innocent people don't normally run, Jason."

"I'm not speaking to you then until I speak with a lawyer," the man replied, gasping.

"That's fine," Charlie said, wiping the blood from his nose. "But regardless of whether you've killed someone or not, you have most certainly assaulted an FBI agent. The federal government doesn't look too kindly on that. You're going to need Perry Mason to get you out of this. Now get up, and move!"

Charlie marched Jason Richardson out of the building to his car, placed him in the back, and locked the door.

Now he needed to contact Valerie, but he'd catch his breath for a moment. Then, he'd hopefully be able to tell his partner that he'd caught the killer once and for all.

CHAPTER TWENTY TWO

The sprawling cornfield looked like a labyrinth of death to Valerie. The stalks of corn swayed in the breeze, but within it hid something terrible, the man who had attacked her in the apartment building.

She had chased him from that ailing structure only for him to flee into that undulating mass of corn stalks from across the empty street.

Valerie hesitated for a moment before the hypothetical guilt of letting him run back into the public to kill again washed over her.

She had to push on.

She had to enter the cornfield, even though it was the perfect place for an ambush.

As she crossed the threshold and listened, she heard something pushing through the stalks of corn, frantically moving away from her. She readied her revolver and moved in that direction, but as she did so, a growing fear fell across her: Had she been led into a trap?

Will had fallen far behind as Valerie had moved after Owen Edgerton. He was still back there somewhere and was yet to emerge from the apartment building.

She was alone in the cornfield, and the shadows within caused her pulse to race with apprehension.

The man was fast, and she felt as though he was still pulling away from her as the noise lessened in volume with each step. She had to up the pace, not just to keep up, but to catch him.

The wind now increased, fingering its way between the channels of corn. The stalks of corn whispered gently in reply. It was not a benign gentleness. It felt as though the cornfield was commenting, taunting, and welcoming her into its embrace. A welcome that was, in truth, an invitation to dance with death.

Owen Edgerton had already proven how crazed and violent he was back at the apartment building across the street. Valerie felt in his current state, he was capable of anything, including butchering an FBI agent.

It was getting increasingly difficult to know which way he had run as Valerie moved deeper into the field. The corn stalks loomed up above her, almost blotting out the sky, and creating walls of moving green and yellow that confused as much as they mesmerized.

One wrong turn, one wrong decision, could take her in the opposite direction of the suspect, or worse, bring her like a lamb to the slaughter into Owen's trap.

The noise had now ceased. The field settled for a moment into itself like the calm before the storm. Was he now watching her? Was he so far away that she could no longer hear him?

There was no obvious clue to Valerie at first glance.

She stopped where she was, gripped her revolver tightly and now fell back on her skills of detection. She slowed herself down momentarily to take in her environment. The cornfield was made up of channels of corn, which crisscrossed each other making it all too easy to get lost.

Owen could have been anywhere.

But Valerie could see what others could not. One piece of corn was slightly broken, an ear of the plant hanging down further than it should have. That was a tell-tale sign that someone had recently been past there in a hurry.

She moved in that direction, and then stopped and listened.

A dull thud and rustling came from somewhere nearby. To the untrained ear it could have been a deer or another animal, but Valerie felt certain it was in fact the footfall of another human being. But was she prey or predator to them?

Valerie moved towards the footsteps. She felt she was just behind them. But just as she was ready to see the source of those footsteps through the next row of crops, she found nothingness.

The sea of corn whispered around her, like a quiet threat.

Where are you, she thought.

Only whispers from the wind came in return. Only the promise of getting lost or worse. And yet she pressed on. She had to.

She then had to make a decision, shaking the paralysis of fear from her mind. She moved in a direction, being assertive, following a hunch. That hunch took her further into the cornfield's embrace.

The gun in her hand moved with purpose, stretched out in front of her. That was a shield; it offered protection from Owen running around in the dim light of the cornfield. But the shadows played tricks, and Valerie began to wonder if she'd be able to react quickly enough if Owen pounced from an unanticipated angle.

Then... Movement...

She turned to her side and, through the ears of corn, suddenly she saw something moving, a black shape between the stalks. An amorphous shadow, blending in to the dim light. It would have disappeared to the untrained eyes, lost to the nothingness. Not to the trained vision of agent Valerie Law, however.

She watched, staying perfectly still as the shadow moved along the channel of corn near her. Then, just as it was about to pass, Valerie leaped forward, gun outstretched and shouted: "Freeze!"

The shadow stopped.

In the dim light, it turned around slowly.

"Please don't shoot me, Valerie, Charlie would never let me live it down," the voice of Will Cooper said. He stood there, hands up, bruised and out of breath, but doing his best to find Valerie.

She was glad he was with her.

"Holy Jesus, I could have killed you, Will."

"You and Charlie always run to help each other," Will said. "I thought I would give it a try myself."

Will moved to talk again, but Valerie put her finger up ushering him to remain quiet.

Something else had entered into her awareness. Two pinpoints of light, dangling still between the corn, visible just a few feet away over Will's right shoulder.

The gray skies above parted slightly, the wind moved the corn, and the light from above caught what was there, watching.

The two pinpoints of light stared out, and from the mouth beneath them, the sound of mumbling and agitation came.

Valerie recognized the voice, if not the words themselves. The skewed whispers were the same ones Valerie had heard back at the derelict apartment building. The same ones that came from Owen Edgerton's apartment before he attacked.

Valerie would not wait. She would not make the same mistake twice.

She moved her eyes tellingly, and Will gave an expression of recognition. He knew they were not alone.

"Stay here," Valerie whispered almost inaudibly. "Trust me."

She then moved off into the corn to the side, acting as though she hadn't seen the eyes watching her. She just hoped Owen would fall for it.

Will stood frozen to the spot.

Splitting her attention between Will and the person watching him,

Valerie watched as the eyes in the corn moved slightly. As she circled around, the gray outline of an emaciated head and face moved back and forwards erratically, then tilting to the side at an unnatural angle.

Will did not move; Valerie kept an eye on him as she moved out of Owen Edgerton's line of sight. She was close now. But she had to be silent. She pressed her feet as gently as possible into the wet soil as she moved ever nearer to her target.

She just hoped she'd reach the man before he moved against Will.

Valerie could no longer see the man's face, just the back of his head and the outline of his gaunt body. Naked, skin over bone.

Walking silently, she was now almost within arm's reach.

But then the suspect moved. He lurched forward, arms outstretched towards Will.

"Valerie!" Will cried out.

Valerie lunged forward as the man moved with incredible speed for someone so emaciated.

He tried to grab Will, but Valerie came tearing through the wall of corn stalks with purpose and aggression.

She kicked out with her leg, swiping the man's left foot. He lost his balance and stumbled momentarily. Valerie responded by slamming her shoulder into his waist, lifting him up off his feet and then powering him into the wet soil.

The man screamed so loudly, Valerie half expected it to wake the dead.

Will quickly helped, grabbing the man's flailing arms, and between the two of them, they were able to hold him on the ground long enough for Valerie to put cuffs on him.

The man then became an emotional wreck, crying and whimpering like a caged animal on the ground. His eyes darted up at Valerie, and he spat at her, his only means now to do any arm.

"Grab his right arm, Will," Valerie said, puffing, out of breath.

"Okay," and he did.

Getting him out of the cornfield was a task. The man kept trying to break free, mumbling and groaning to himself.

In every way, he was like an animal. And that worried Valerie.

They put him the back of the car and locked the doors.

"I think we should get him medical assistance," Will started.

"He's not the only one."

Valerie held her side. She felt her ribs. They were bruised, but nothing was broken as she had first feared. But she still felt like she'd been through the wars.

"I'll call an ambulance," she said, looking up at the gray sky. "How are you holding up?"

"I'm fine," Will said. "Just a little shaken and sore. Maybe I should take up a martial art."

"It's not a bad idea."

"I was joking, "Will said, wincing as he touched his bruised nose.

"I know," Valerie said. "I just like to humor you."

They got in the car, and Valerie called for an ambulance and a patrol car.

Both Valerie and Will tried to speak with Owen in the back of the car to keep him conscious. He seemed to be in an almost catatonic state now.

Valerie hoped the ambulance would arrive quickly.

As they waited, the cornfield moved as one back and forward slightly in the wind. Valerie never wanted to go into a place like that again.

She felt as though this case was destined to push her to her limits. If it pushed her much further, she worried that she would come apart at the seams.

CHAPTER TWENTY THREE

The killer desired nothing more than to sleep and to rest as he trudged through the countryside. But he knew he could never *truly* be at peace. The woman wouldn't let him. The same woman, the same face that haunted his waking hours and his restless dreams.

The vision of it, the smile upon it, it all brought him to a place of fear and anger. And that was a potent cocktail inside the head of a psychotic individual.

Rest, he thought. *I need rest.*

He'd found himself on the outskirts of a small town again. He was wandering away from the highways and main roads. He was following seldom walked paths, trails that wound through patches of wasted ground and forgotten, overgrown dirt tracks that had once served a purpose, only to have been reclaimed by the trees and bushes.

He thought staying out of populated areas was his best bet to avoid detection.

It wasn't the police he feared or the FBI. He feared that *she* would find him.

He could evade her by sticking to such places. She'd find it difficult to locate him. At least, that was his hope. But he had already been tracked down by her in such a place. Masquerading as a jogger out in the morning.

But he wasn't stupid. He knew who she was, the disguise didn't fool him. He could see she had the same eyes. He'd put his knife in her and enjoyed the thought that he had robbed her of another chance to torture him.

She was the bringer of death. This he knew. There was a symmetry in bringing death to her. And he couldn't think of anyone else who deserved the abyss more.

These thoughts swirled around his mind like a maelstrom. He steadied himself and tried to focus on staying hidden from her.

Scanning the small winding path he now found himself on, he was exhausted. He knew he had to find somewhere to hide and sleep. If he didn't, he wouldn't be fresh and rejuvenated if, or rather *when* that woman would find him again.

As if called by it, an old work shed came into view nearby, just to the side of an old, seldom-traveled trail. It looked beat up. As abandoned and beat up as he had been by society, by her. At least in his eyes.

He moved over to the work shed and found that, although the door was locked, a crooked window had long since relented to the elements. He climbed inside to the darkness, the wooden frame of the window scraping against his hands, only to find worn machinery. Somewhere between those old scraps of metal and tools long forgotten, he found a patch of ground on which to lay.

He lay down on the floor, the coldness of it seeping into his body. He tried to close his eyes, but the intrusion into his mind began all over again. The woman's face was clear in his thoughts.

The man believed that she was somehow attacking him telepathically. She was invading his thoughts. He had to stop her. He had to...

The only way was to kill, to bludgeon, to eviscerate... Only then could he be free of her. Of her taunting. It didn't matter how many times it would take. It didn't matter to the killer how many times she would resurrect and come back. Eventually, he would triumph. She could only manifest herself as long there was energy around her. That was his theory. In his paranoid mind, the killer thought she would run out of energy. She would cease being able to resurrect and manifest, and he could finally rest.

But not now.

He closed his eyes again and the same face flashed before them. With all his willpower, he fought the intrusion.

He wished he had never listened to his doctor. The medications had stopped the visions for some time, but he saw now that those same medications were part of the conspiracy against him. Everyone was in the employ of the face, of that woman. They were all in on it together. They wanted to deaden his senses with the medications so they could more easily come for him.

Well, he wouldn't let them. He would resist. And each time he saw that face, he would destroy it.

Exhaustion now replaced the terrible image that had haunted him for days on end. The coldness of the work shed dropped into the background of his senses. Something comforting then came to him.

Finally, he was able to replace the intrusive face momentarily with another. One that was kind and caring. One that he loved. One that would understand that he had to kill.

It was the face of his mother.

He slowly drifted off in the care of that memory. She would see him off to sleep, and he would sleep soundly at least for a while. Because he felt protected. Because he felt his mother would look over him.

His last thought before sleep finally took him completely, was that he'd do anything to think of his mother and only her. To never see the other woman's face ever again. He knew that would mean killing her again the next day, and the day after that.

Over and over until the nightmare ended.

CHAPTER TWENTY FOUR

Valerie stood next to the ambulance. The red and blue lights bathed her in their alternating glow. She was watching as the man she had chased through the cornfields, Owen Edgerton, was being treated by paramedics.

He was malnourished, and he was suffering from tachycardia. Whether this was brought on by the chase through the cornfields or by his severe lack of food and water consumption, Valerie did not know.

Owen was supposed to have received a wellness check by authorities two weeks earlier. But that check never came to pass due to their resources being stretched and Owen not being seen as a priority.

Will approached with a coffee in hand. "Here you go," he said, handing the coffee to Valerie.

She took it and then took a deep sip. "Thanks, Will," she said, looking thoughtfully at the emaciated figure of Owen sitting up in the back of the ambulance.

She couldn't help but feel sorry for the man. He was suffering from neglect, dehydration, and lack of food. All of this had compounded his already profound mental health issues.

If ever there was a poster child for someone not in control of their actions, it was Owen Edgerton.

"Do I have to say anything?" Will said, nursing the bruise on his face that he had suffered during his altercation with the suspect.

"I know I don't have a full profile yet," Will said. "But I don't think he's the killer."

"I have doubts about that myself," Valerie said, sipping her coffee. "He's too erratic. By the state of his condition, he's been malnourished for some time, but his psychotic breakdown is pumping him full of adrenaline. So much so he was able to contend with both of us..."

"He's in a frenzied, adrenaline-filled state where decision making is completely compromised," she continued. "His actions are impulsive, yes, but *too* impulsive for our killer. Owen Edgerton couldn't remain hidden. He'd be in a daze, walk into traffic, or be found stumbling around the streets mumbling to himself. He's so mentally compromised at this point, I don't think he could even properly dress himself."

"You might be right," Will sighed.

A police officer walked over towards Will and Valerie. "Agent Law?"

"Yes?"

"We've interviewed someone who claims they live in there," the cop pointed to the dilapidated apartment building. "A neighbor named Jon Brannigan. He says Owen hasn't left the building for weeks. Jon claims he's been bringing him food and water, but he hasn't ventured out further. He even places Owen in the building during two of the murders. He is a junkie, though... So I..."

Valerie hated that term.

"Even people afflicted with addiction can tell the truth," she said.

"Uh... Yeah."

"Well, that settles it then," Will said.

Valerie only needed this as validation. Her profiling skill had already told her Owen Edgerton was probably not the killer.

"Thank you, Officer," Valerie said. "I'll have someone liaise with you to run over his alibi."

The officer nodded and returned to the ambulance.

"If he isn't the killer, we do have one piece of evidence now, though, that is pointing us in a good direction."

"And what's that?" Valerie said, feeling forlorn.

"Look at that man," Will said. "He clearly wasn't ready to be released. The administrator back at the Wendel Institute might have been trying to get as many people back into the general population as quickly as possible. His intentions might have been good, but whoever he's brought in to evaluate each patient, they've severely let him down."

"Catastrophic errors have clearly been made. Owen Edgerton should not have been released to his own volition. He's paranoid. He's violent. And all of this comes from a profound confusion brought about by some extreme psychosis."

Will looked over at the emaciated figure in the ambulance again. Paramedics had put an oxygen mask over his face and were now getting ready to transport him to a hospital.

"He needs treatment. How anyone could think he was ready for the general population, I don't know," Will said, trailing off.

"So you think it's feasible then," Valerie said, following on from will's thought. "That the institute has released people who may be violent? An individual, perhaps, who could even perhaps become a serial killer?"

"If he wasn't already a serial killer before he went in that place," Will said.

But there was a growing hesitation in Valerie's mind. Will's observation was correct. The condition that Owen Edgerton was in should have filled her with more confidence that the real killer was among the names on the list the administrator had given them.

But she couldn't shake her intuitions.

A theory about the killer's identity was formulating in her mind. It would turn the investigation on its head, and so she didn't want to be too rash in her judgment She needed to discuss it first with Will and Charlie to see if they agreed that she was on the right track. In the end, the last word would be hers, but with lives at stake and a possible countdown to the killer going dark for a while, she couldn't afford to make the wrong move.

CHAPTER TWENTY FIVE

Valerie had struggled to keep her eyes open as she drove through the evening rain. Will was trying to keep the conversation going as best he could, but Valerie could tell that he was as exhausted as she was.

Pulling into the parking lot at the Mallgreen Motel, she could feel her bones ache from head to toe. It had been two days since she'd been to sleep. She'd never felt so exhausted.

She was threadbare, and staying up any longer was going to put her and her team's health at risk.

But Charlie had messaged as they traveled for her and Will to meet him at the motel bar for a quick debrief with each other. Valerie was pretty certain that also meant he'd be drinking a stiff bourbon. She couldn't face alcohol, not when she was so shattered. But she did agree that they needed to catch each other up on how they were getting on with the names on the Wendel list.

After checking in and booking two rooms for her and Will, the two tired investigators traipsed through the tacky motel lobby and then through to a small bar on the other side of the lot. A fake moose head sat above the door.

She entered the bar feeling like she had been there before. Chasing serial killers had taken her around the country, and she invariably found herself sleeping in rundown places such as the Mallgreen Motel during each case. It could have been any motel in any part of the country. Even the bartender seemed like a cookie-cutter image through the fog of Valerie's exhaustion.

Will pointed to the half empty wooden bar where Charlie sat slumped on a stool, glass in hand and looking like he'd fall asleep if someone put relaxing music on the juke box.

Will waved and Charlie nodded. He just about managed a smile.

Valerie and Will walked over to him. She saw some bruises and cuts on her partner's face.

"Get into an altercation with someone, Charlie?" Valerie asked. "Please tell me you had better luck than we did."

Charlie seemed surprised to see that they too were battered and bruised.

He said: "You two look how I feel."

"What happened?" Valerie asked, concerned.

Charlie sighed and took a sip of his bourbon as if he needed the belt to face recounting his day.

"I spent all day chasing a guy names Jason Richardson. Real piece of work. Violent and twisted."

"And?" Valerie said, hopefully.

"Val," Charlie answered. "If he'd been the guy, I'd have contacted you immediately."

"But I thought you said you arrested him in your message?"

"I did," Charlie said. "The guy bolted and we got into a fight. I still brought him in."

"How do you know it wasn't him?" Will asked. "An alibi?"

"Yeah," Charlie sighed taking another sip from his glass. "Not only did the people at the bar vouch that he'd been there a couple of the nights when the victims were murdered, there was security footage from the bar to back that up from the owner."

"And this Richardson guy did that to your face?" Valerie asked.

"The guy's a scumbag," Charlie answered. "I'm sure he's done something bad, and that's why he ran. What that something is, I don't know. Either way, he's going to jail for assaulting an FBI agent. I'll let someone else process him and figure out why he was running."

Charlie looked at Valerie and Will. "What happened with you two?"

"We had to chase a man through a cornfield," Will said.

"Like Children of the Corn?" Charlie asked, grinning with tired eyes.

Charlie always knew how bring levity to the darkest of situations.

"I love Stephen King as much as anyone, Charlie," Valerie said. "But wrestling with a psychotic in a cornfield wasn't exactly on my bucket list."

Charlie finished his drink. "Would you two like a drink?"

"I think if I drank anything I'd pass out before I made it to my room," Valerie said.

"The man we were chasing is Owen Edgerton," Valerie said. "The guy was in the throes of a persecution delusion. Heavily paranoid. He'd stopped washing and eating properly. He could barely string a sentence together."

"That doesn't sound like the killer to me," Charlie said. "This one is a weird mix of being in control and not at the same time."

"The guy we're looking for undoubtedly suffers from a profound psychiatric illness, but he is not so far gone he can't take care of himself."

"That's my feeling, too," Will said. "We've taken a DNA swab to match it to a hair forensics found at one of the murder scenes. But I doubt it's a match."

"I do have a theory," Valerie said, hesitating.

"Well that's good," said Charlie. "Because I'm out of ideas right now, other than just going through this list until we get beaten on by more violent inmates from Ward 17 of the Wendel Institute."

"I mentioned to Valerie," said Will, "that, at least we know from these two individuals that the Wendel Institute hasn't been doing their proper diligence. These are people who should never have been released without heavy oversight."

Valerie saw Charlie looking at her.

He scratched his cheek and then said: "Why do I feel like you're about to tell me something I don't really want to hear."

"I've started to put a proper profile together for the killer based on everything we've learned about the murder scenes, the victims, and inferred personality traits from his actions. I'm beginning to wonder if he's not on the list at all."

"Why do you say that?" Charlie asked.

"It first struck me," Valerie said. "When we were talking to the first person on the list..."

"Tarron Saelim?" Charlie asked.

"Yes," Valerie said. "It was when he talked about medications."

"What about them?" asked Will.

"It made me think about the thin veneer between being stable and being not. He talked about how he was trying to stay in a stable frame of mind. Working out, taking meds etc."

"Mr. Saelim went from being someone in the grips of the deepest psychosis to being someone who was reliable and was sane. A big part of that was because of the support he got from his sister. All that together, his treatment, his sister, he was using all of that to stop going backwards. It kept him out of institutes, at least as a full-time patient."

"What does this have to do with the killer?" Charlie asked, slouching on the bar stool as if he'd fall off it, exhausted, at any moment.

Valerie said: "What if the killer we are hunting is the reverse of Mr.

Saelim? What if he's someone who *has* been stable, always. He's been taking his meds. He's been someone who has until this point in his life never even harmed another person. He's had all the supports in place, he's had the routines, he's had the medications, he's perhaps even had his family helping to look after him. Then suddenly that's gone for some reason."

"Mr. Saelim was concerned about the idea that he would go back to being unstable, and that would have happened to him if he didn't have the support networks in his life. Maybe that's happened to the killer. The walls have fallen down, a delusion has built up, and now he's unleashing his brutality almost impulsively. He could have been pretty well adjusted before this."

"That's a bit of a stretch Valerie," Will said. "You know about the patterns of escalation. Serial killers normally start with animals and then move their way up to people. It could take years, but there are normally warning signs."

"I'm not saying there were no warning signs with this guy," Valerie said. "But what if he was like Mr. Saelim? What if he was on medication and then a dramatic moment threw him out of that loop. Cut him loose. I mean just look at Edgerton."

"I don't see the connection?" Charlie said.

"Owen Edgerton was supposed to have wellness checks," Valerie said. "He didn't get them. He didn't have the same network of support that Mr. Saelim had in his life. The disparity is clear."

"But just because someone doesn't have the support they need doesn't mean they become a serial killer," Will said.

"I know. Thousands of people go through that and never harm a fly. But there's always one. There's always someone who is a little out of the box. Different. In all of the bad ways. Sometimes it's a powder keg situation and all that's needed is someone to light the blue paper. We could be looking at a spontaneous serial killer here and not someone with a history of violence."

"So what does this mean?" Charlie asked. "Are you saying then that the killer was never at Wendel Institute? We're wasting our time with the list?"

"I'm saying that he may never have been institutionalized at any point, anywhere in his life," Valerie said. "He maybe was given medications by a doctor. He was able to stay in the community and he seemed stable like Mr. Saelim. And then some traumatic event altered that and turned him into something like Owen Edgerton, only worse.

It's just a working idea."

"The question is," said Charlie. "What do we do with that?"

"We sleep," Valerie said. "God knows we need it now more than ever. Local law enforcement are on the lookout. We need to rest for a night or we'll make a critical mistake from exhaustion. Jackson Weller wouldn't be happy about that."

Valerie's phone suddenly buzzed. She pulled it out and looked down at the caller ID. It was Tom.

She was so shattered. She didn't want to speak to him, but she knew that she had to. She hadn't spoken to him in days. Not since she had so abruptly left his family home.

She made her excuses and left Will and Charlie at the bar and then answered the phone once she was outside.

"Valerie," Tom said from the other end of the line. His usually cheery voice was gone and he sounded frustrated and sad.

"Tom," Valerie offered. "I'm sorry. I've been caught up in this case."

"I thought you would be," Tom said. "You know I try to support your career. I get it, you sometimes need to go at a moment's notice. But the way you acted... Do you know my parents are now questioning whether you're the right person for me? They're wondering if you're stable or not? Why did you run out on us like that?"

"I told you, I had a case," Valerie stated unconvincingly.

"But you were heading for the door before you knew anything about that," Tom said. "It was like you were about to have a full-blown panic attack. And then you wouldn't let me be there to help you."

"I'm sorry, Tom." Valerie said. "I kept thinking about my family while we sat with your family. I know it wasn't the time or place for that, but I just couldn't help it. The thoughts just came in, and I didn't know what to do with them. I messed up, Tom. Things got on top of me emotionally and ruined something that was supposed to be a big deal for you. Please say sorry to your parents for me."

"I can smooth it over," Tom said. "But why don't you come back and stay here, if you're in the area."

"Oh, I'm in a motel miles away. I haven't slept for two days," Valerie said.

"I see," Tom replied. He sighed, and his voice changed to being more understanding. "Valerie, just look after yourself. I love you."

"I know," she said. "And I love you, too. Maybe once this case is finished I can come back over and see your family."

"We'll see," Tom said. "Just get some rest. I'll speak to you tomorrow. Good night."

"Good night, Tom," Valerie said.

Valerie walked, numb, back into the bar.

"Everything okay?" Charlie asked.

"I think we all need to get some rest," Will said. "You the most, Valerie."

"Would you two please stop fussing," Valerie resisted. "It was Tom. Everything is fine. We're fine."

"You're only a few miles from his mom and dad's house," Charlie remarked. "Why don't you go there for the night and we'll meet up with you in the morning. It's got to be better than this rundown motel. Hell, if there's a cozy room going in an old townhouse, I'll take it." The joke fell on to silence.

"I'd rather stay here," Valerie said succinctly. She knew she had lied to Tom about how far the motel was from his family's home. But she couldn't face that happy family. Not now. Not with so much on her mind. Not with so much to lose if she were unable to keep it together.

If Tom's family thought she was a bit unstable with how she had acted when nearly having a panic attack, Valerie shuddered to think how they would react if she had some sort of full blown mental breakdown brought on by stress.

She felt so frazzled, she couldn't rule that out from happening. Not when she was starting to believe she had the same illness that Suzie and her mother had.

"Tomorrow," Valerie said, pushing everything else to the back of her mind. "We'll work on a new profile and we'll have to try and predict his next move if we're to have any chance of stopping his next kill and catching him. We can send some other agents to go over some of the names on the Wendel list while we work on the new profile."

"Okay," Will said, reluctantly. "But I still think that list is our best hope of finding the killer."

"Maybe it is," Valerie said. "But we need to entertain the idea that the killer isn't on it."

Valerie said good night to her partners and walked back to her room.

Exhausted, she fell onto her bed, hoping that the next day would bring a new revelation in the case.

CHAPTER TWENTY SIX

Sally Renfield had been an Uber driver for 16 months. Her car moved through the hot night onto its next destination. It hadn't been the best of nights. So far, Sally had only two decent hires taking her in and out of the area. The rest were all smaller local ones. Other than that, it had been quiet.

She'd also had some obnoxious passengers in the car as well. Some of them drunk, others just being rude. Sally could never understand why people thought it was okay to be so disrespectful to someone just doing their job. Especially when that someone was trying to get them to their destination as quickly and as safely as possible.

Her next hire was a couple of miles away. She was out on some back roads moving along at speed, the uneven road grumbling beneath the tires. She hadn't taken her car to the shop, and there was an almost imperceptible clunking noise on the left side of the vehicle as it moved over the rough surface. She had a bad feeling that noise would get worse and she'd be yet again forking out cash she didn't have to keep herself on the road and making a living.

Sally was tired. She would make this her last hire for the night. After that, she'd go grab some coffee with a couple of other drivers she often met up with during quieter nights.

The road she had most recently turned down was particularly eerie looking. Some of the turns were so sharp it was as if the road almost double backed onto itself. In Sally's mind it reminded her of the body of a snake, coiling through the darkness.

There were no lights, and only her headlights to catch the occasional reflective sign or road marking to let her know she wasn't veering off course into a ditch.

Those roads were not meant for cars. They had been built a couple of hundred years earlier for horses and carts. This made them narrow and particularly hazardous for fast moving cars.

Sally didn't like those back roads; they creeped her out, but she had to go where the money was, and that road was a short cut.

Up ahead in the darkness, trees lined each side of the road as if escorting it into the bleak night. In places, they looked like crooked figures watching Sally as she moved between them. A wall of twisted black and green lit only by the shadows cast by Sally's car headlights.

That is why what she saw stood out so much against that wall of still woodland. It was the flash of something white, bent over and running, with eyes glinting in the dark. It darted across the road in front of the car. Sally slammed on her brakes, passing it, and the thing scrambled and then collapsed into the undergrowth by the side of the car.

Sally didn't need to take a second look as her car screeched to a halt. She knew what it was. The form was distinct. It was man. And her tired mind was uncertain about why he had fallen. Had she hit him?

"Oh my God, oh my God, oh my God," she said repeatedly to herself in a panic.

The engine of her car purred beneath the blanket of clouds and stars above. It growled like an animal, waiting for another victim.

Sally didn't know what to do. She had a growing sense of dread in her stomach. An understandable one.

First, she was worried for the man. But she was also heavily concerned for her livelihood. Hitting someone with her car could easily result in her license being revoked.

She wanted to help and make sure that she hadn't just done something terrible because she was so tired. But, she was out there on her own. She had the worry of leaving her car. Cabbies and Uber drivers were always warning each other about scams and robberies. Sally was still hardly a veteran, but she'd heard of people faking accidents. The driver would then get out, check on the person and someone else would steal their car or money.

Sally was already behind with her rent. She couldn't really afford for something like that to happen to her. Most of her hires paid digitally, but she still had a couple of hundred bucks on her. And she most certainly couldn't afford to have her car stolen.

She looked down at her phone, but there was no reception. She couldn't even call for help. But this didn't surprise her. That area was populated with undulating hills and on the back roads reception was patchy at best.

She cursed herself for having taken the shortcut just to make a few extra bucks and save gas.

Then the strangeness of it all finally made itself apparent as she looked over her shoulder to where the man may have been lying.

"Why was he running across the road in the middle of nowhere?" she asked herself out loud.

Despite her misgivings, there was nothing she could do. She had to help. She got out of the car and hoped beyond hope that the man had just fallen off balance, was now on his feet, and continuing on his way.

But deep under her skin, she felt that this wouldn't be the case.

She closed the door of the car behind her and locked it and looked apprehensively at the trees around her in the dark, wondering if she was about to be robbed. But the trees just silently stared back.

Sally took a few steps to the rear of the car. It was difficult to see, her red taillight casting a dim hue on the shadows.

"Hello?" she said out loud. "Are you okay?"

She peered towards the edge of the road, taking one more step. That was when she saw it: a sneakered foot on the edge of the thick grass. The man was there, and he was still lying crumpled on the ground, partially obscured by the thick undergrowth.

Sally was now convinced that he was injured, and that she was responsible.

She moved ever closer. "Hello?" and then stopped, awaiting a response. No response came.

An impulse in her mind made her want to go back to her car and drive off. She was ashamed of that. She had always been brought up to help those in need, and to take responsibility for your mistakes. Why then was every fiber in her being telling her to turn around and leave?

She shook that thought and kept moving forward.

As she neared, she could see the full body of the man. He was lying on his face, curled up with his hands covering his eyes.

He was conscious. Sally was grateful for that.

But he was saying something over and over in a whispered voice.

"Are you okay?" she asked again. But he only continued whispering.

She strained to listen.

"Not hear, not hear, not hear," is what it sounded like.

She started to think that he had been concussed by the fall or that he was drunk, staggering around the back roads

"Let me help you up," she said.

"Not hear, not hear, not hear," he said again and again, muffled.

Sally was now a few feet from her car. She looked over her shoulder to it as though it were shelter from an oncoming storm. Then she turned back to the man.

She didn't know what to do. She couldn't just leave him. She had to help him or take him to a hospital.

She finally reached him and leaned down to see if he had any obvious injuries. But she couldn't see any blood.

Then she worried that the reason he was shielding his face with his hands was because he had hurt his eyes in the fall.

"Let me look, please," she said, gently.

Reaching down, she touched the man's hands and pulled them away from his face.

That was when the voice became more legible.

His eyes opened, manic and wild. And Sally finally realized that she had misheard him. He wasn't saying "not hear." He was saying "not her."

Sally Renfield didn't have enough time to understand this.

The man clenched his teeth and pushed up with something long and sharp he'd pulled from his pocket.

The knife cut deep into Sally's stomach. She felt an indescribable agony as the knife was then moved up in one quick motion like the man was gutting a fish.

She bled out there on the side of the road, collapsing on the ground as the crooked trees watched silently in the night.

CHAPTER TWENTY SEVEN

Valerie stirred in the morning. She looked at the clock in the motel room. She was shocked that the night had passed without her usual tossing and turning, something she had been doing increasingly in recent months.

She didn't remember stirring at all; this was a welcome reprieve from her usual nightly routine of sleeping in fits and starts.

Valerie stared up at the motel room ceiling. A shard of light cast across it from a gap in the blinds nearby.

She knew how truly exhausted she must have been, because her dreams were normally places where the pressures of her life truly found her. Unnerving fragments of her daytime existing, cast as nightmarish forms while she slept.

Last night was the closest she'd had to a restful sleep in some time, and she was surprised that it had happened in such a rundown motel room.

She breathed out a sigh; it was one that did not carry anxiety. For once, she had forgotten the apprehension on her mind. Her worries had melted away. No thoughts of her mother or sister, no guilt over her relationship with Tom, and no agonizing over catching a serial killer before they killed again.

Valerie's mind had finally given her some respite. For that brief moment, she was just a woman enjoying the quiet serenity of some peaceful rest.

But then that rest was abruptly shattered.

Three loud knocks came at the door.

"Val, it's Charlie," the voice said, muffled by the thin barrier of the motel door. "Are you up?"

As if it had been hiding in some subterranean part of her psyche, waiting to reassert itself, all of Valerie's worries seeped back into her awareness at the sound of Charlie's voice, washing over her like a tsunami.

She almost didn't want to open the door, but she knew she had to. She could hear it in Charlie's voice.

Something bad had happened.

Valerie pulled on her clothes and opened the door. The early morning sun shone through the gap, making it difficult to see as her eyes adapted to its brilliance.

Both Will and Charlie were standing there in the sun, but they were not smiling with the weather.

"What's happened?" Valerie asked.

"There's been another murder," Will said, looking still tired and unrested.

"Nearby?" Valerie asked.

"Yeah," said Charlie. "About a half an hour drive."

"Give me a few minutes to get ready and we'll head to the scene."

Charlie nodded. "We'll get you out in the parking lot."

Valerie closed the door and then closed her eyes. All too soon, the evil of the world was back in her life, and it was her duty to go out and meet it.

*

The crime scene was on the back roads just outside Indianapolis. Valerie, Charlie, and Will arrived as quickly as they could.

The road was isolated from nearby towns by stretches of woodland and empty farmland. But Valerie wasn't surprised by the fact that the murder had taken place there.

"We should start to think about where the killer is moving," she said to Will and Charlie as they walked towards the cordoned off scene.

Several officers stood waiting.

"Yeah," Charlie replied. "I have noticed that it's mainly been rural areas or wasted ground where the last few victims have been found. All apart from the first victim in the hospital parking lot."

Valerie stopped for a second. A thought buzzed through her mind. *The nurse...* She mused for a moment that the first victim's location was different. Perhaps that was for a reason. But that thought was quickly interrupted by the line of cops buzzing around the patch of road.

"Agent Law with the FBI," Valerie said, feeling like she was in a continual loop of introducing herself at death scenes.

"Nice to meet you," a younger officer said in an all too cordial tone for a horrific murder scene.

A couple of the other cops beside him rolled their eyes as if he was kissing up.

"Can you show us the body, please?" Charlie asked.

The young officer walked them further along the road where an old black SUV sat motionless. There, not far behind the car, was another young woman cut down in her prime, lying there like an island of death, a large pool of congealed blood having soaked the earth and grass around her body.

She had one large wound running up from her navel to her chest.

Her eyes were closed yet again.

"She looks vaguely like the other women victims," Will said, his voice grim.

"Yeah she does," Valerie agreed.

"Looks just like one wound this time rather than a frenzied attack," Charlie observed.

"It does," Valerie agreed, "but we'll only know for sure once an autopsy is carried out."

Will took out a handkerchief and patted his mouth. Valerie knew by now that this meant he felt sick or overcome. She had to remind herself from time to time that this was still relatively new for him, seeing people like this in the flesh.

She patted his back. "You okay?"

"Yes," Will replied. "I was just thinking that he wouldn't need to carry out a frenzied attack as such. The eyes are closed again, so he obviously feels some sort of remorse afterwards. This must come quickly after the murder, otherwise he wouldn't be here to close each victim's eyes."

"And he wouldn't need to repeatedly stab this woman as she clearly died quickly from the immediate wound," Charlie agreed.

Valerie looked at the skid marks in the road behind the car. She noticed that they started before where her body was, stretching out to where the car was sitting.

"She must have thought she hit him, stopped and then got to out to check."

"A good deed goes punished once again," Will sighed. "But how are we going to stop him from doing this to another young woman?"

Valerie looked around at the isolated road and took a deep breath.

"You think it's something to do with the location?" Charlie asked, watching his partner.

"Possibly…" Valerie pulled out her phone and brought up a map of the area with the murder locations already marked. She zoomed out with her fingers and thought for a moment.

She could feel her pulse start to race.

"So far, we've thought this guy is driven only by the fact that these women look similar," Valerie restated.

"Agreed," said Will.

"But what if there's something else we've missed?" Valerie held up the phone with the map on it to her colleagues.

"My word," Will said.

Valerie ran her finger from the first murder in the hospital parking lot, to the body in the barn, then to the wasted ground where the jogger was murdered, and finally to that point where the Uber driver had been killed.

"That looks," she said confidently, "very much like a direction."

"He's using back roads and countryside," Charlie observed. "But he's actually going somewhere. But where?"

"My guess is he's going home," Valerie said. "He needs to rest and get out of this constant murder cycle, but he just can't help himself."

"I have an idea," Charlie offered. "Let's assume he's on foot. He can only cover about twenty miles at max, especially given this terrain. Let's see if any of the names on the Wendel list match anywhere in the direction the killer is heading."

"Excellent idea," Will said.

"Agreed," replied Valerie. "Let me check."

Valerie still preferred field work, but she had to give it up to the tech guys. They did make some of her work easier. She was able to quickly filter the database of addresses from the Wendel list on her phone and have them appear on the map.

"Bingo," Charlie said looking over Valerie's shoulder.

"Looks like there are two addresses," she said. "We'll need to split up."

"Okay, I'm with you," Will said.

Valerie smiled. "Not so fast, Will. I want you to go with Charlie this time. We need a profiler at each address in case something important comes up."

Will and Charlie agreed and made their way to their cars.

It was a solid suggestion, but Valerie had another reason to want Will to go with Charlie. She didn't want another repeat of the near accident on the road.

She was starting to doubt her ability to keep her mind clear enough to protect those around her. And an agent without that ability would soon find themselves pulled from service if they didn't get themselves back on track.

Valerie knew she could do that. But she just needed a little time.

That was something she didn't have. She got in her car and headed out to one of the addresses directly on the killer's warpath.

CHAPTER TWENTY EIGHT

Valerie was only a few minutes out from the address when the text appeared.

The message asked Valerie to contact her boss Jackson Weller when appropriate.

She was positive that only meant one thing: If it had to do with the case, her boss would have contacted her right away. He wouldn't have just sent a message.

That could only mean he wanted to discuss something else, and Valerie was pretty sure what that was.

She pulled over for a moment and gazed at the message on her phone with dread in her heart. Had Jackson finally found out something about her father's whereabouts?

There was no time for hesitancy. She knew that she should have left the call until after visiting the next suspect as it could affect her mindset.

But some itches had to be scratched, and finding her father was one of them.

She called him quickly, using hands-free and getting the car back on the road moving towards the destination on the map.

The phone rang momentarily before being answered. Valerie was so nervous she didn't give him a chance to say hello.

"Jackson?"

"Eh, Agent Law," Jackson said. "How's the investigation proceeding?"

"I'm en route to another suspect as we speak," Valerie said. She didn't want to update him on how trying it had been. Not yet. The last thing she needed was for her boss to think she wasn't dealing with the case's most difficult aspects.

"Good, good" Jackson said. There was a silence for a moment. Valerie could tell he was waiting to say something.

"There's something you want to say to me, isn't there, Jackson?" Valerie asked. She was frightened what the answer to that would be.

"Valerie," Jackson said, his voice as serious as stone. "I've used

119

every means at my disposal to help find your dad. But it's as if your father disappeared off the face of the earth. There's no clue as to his whereabouts. Not that I can find at least. He's never drawn a paycheck. He's never been seen by any of his family, though he was estranged from most of them in any case. No matches coming up with photographs online. He hasn't been seen or heard from in twenty years. Nothing."

He hesitated for a moment and then cleared his throat before continuing. "Valerie, you know as well as I do as an agent, there really are only two conclusions to draw from that."

Valerie didn't want to accept what he was saying. But it was true. If Jackson felt he had exhausted all avenues open to him, it really did mean that her father had vanished.

"I know, Jackson," she said. "Either my dad has been using a different name or identity, or..." She couldn't bring herself to finish the sentence.

Immediately, she remembered him patting her on the head when she was six years old for doing well at her dance class. Why that memory, and why now, she didn't know.

Jackson stated the horrible truth for her: "It's likely that something has happened to him in the past, and that's why there's no trace of him."

"I know." It was all Valerie could say.

"I'm sorry I don't have more positive news, Valerie. If anything else turns up, I'll let you know."

"No, Jackson," Valerie said. "I'm just glad you're willing to help." There was a slight buzz on the line for a moment.

"I just wanted to contact you to say I could run an international check, see if he's in another country? It's a long shot, but it might turn something up," Jackson said. "But I didn't want to dig further without your approval. I know this is deeply personal for you."

"I really appreciate that, Chief," Valerie said. "That would be great, though... I know it's unlikely, but I'm just holding onto the hope that there's always a small chance he's still alive and well in the US and he's just slipped under the radar somehow."

"That's true," Jackson sounded as though he was trying to be reassuring, but the doubt in his voice was clear to Valerie.

"Thanks, Jackson."

"Are you going to be okay?" he asked, care in his voice.

"I will be," Valerie said. But that was a lie. Valerie couldn't promise she would be fine. Finding her father would have not only let her heal a childhood wound when he ran out on her, but her father might have been able to get more out of her mom than she ever could.

There was still the matter of some of the things she wrote to Valerie. They needed to be explained. Valerie couldn't go through life wondering about details of her life her mother had scribbled down in her messages. She had to have answers.

"I better go, Jackson. I'm nearly at the next suspect's house."

"Okay," Jackson said. "But if things are getting on top of you..."

"I wish people would stop saying that," Valerie opined. "I'm fine. And I will remain *fine*."

"Alright. Keep me up to date. And call if you need anything. Good luck."

"Bye."

The call ended and Valerie tried to process what Jackson had told her. She wanted to think it over. She wanted to keep going on the road, set out and get on her father's trail: find out where he was and what had happened to him.

But duty called. And when it did, Valerie had to answer.

The killer could still have been on the list. And that had to be a priority. For all she knew, she was on the way to the killer's home right now.

She had to stay sharp.

But for the first time in many years, Valerie didn't want it to be a priority. She wanted to heal the wounds of her threadbare family, make them better, and in return, make herself whole again.

CHAPTER TWENTY NINE

Charlie had a growing feeling that he was entering into the lion's den. He and Will were on a trail that wound its way along a country path between thick patches of woodland and then mingled with bushes and large ferns. Some of them were so high, Charlie's line of sight was completely obscured.

"Who lives with no road access nowadays?" Charlie grumbled.

"It sounds rather picturesque to me," Will said. "I just hope this suspect... Robert Brimley, is as calm as the surroundings."

"Calm?" Charlie said. "I feel like we're walking into an ambush or a horror film. You know, one of those cabin in the woods type situations."

The two men continued down the path, regardless.

"You mustn't let your previous experiences make you paranoid, Charlie," Will offered. "That's not exactly healthy thinking for you. Paranoid approaches never are."

"Healthy thinking or not, Will," Charlie said. "Being wary of situations where I can't even see where I'm going has kept me alive in the army and in the field with the FBI. If that's paranoid, then count me in."

"Fair enough," Will replied. "I think Valerie would probably agree with you."

"I don't know what Valerie's thinking these days," Charlie said mournfully. "She's always been so together. But it feels recently like she's unsure of herself and the things around her. Haven't you felt that?"

Will didn't answer immediately. Their footsteps crunched on the undergrowth that had partially reclaimed that section of narrow trail.

"I don't want to believe it," Will finally said. "But I'm beginning to worry that she is in need of an extended break from the FBI."

"I wouldn't be that drastic," Charlie said, surprised. "If I thought things were that bad I wouldn't be confident to have her as my partner. But other than my wife, there's no one I trust as much as Val. I just think maybe she needs our help with some of her family stuff. I just wish she'd let us in more."

"We have to be careful when it comes to families, Charlie," Will said. "When there are deep traumatic familial wounds, they can cause erratic behavior even in someone as seemingly stable and together as Valerie is."

"So you don't think we should try to help?"

"I didn't say that," Will replied. "She's our colleague, our friend, and I want us to help as much as possible. But if we push too much, we'll be in danger of pushing her further away. When we were going to Owen Edgerton's, she grew *very* irritated over my attempts to talk to her about how she was doing. For now, I think it's best that we let her open up to us. We can keep her close so that we can help when needed and so that we can watch over her the way she watches over us."

"The irony there is that she's on her own right now chasing up another name from the list," Charlie said. "We're not exactly keeping her close."

"I know, I meant figuratively."

The path altered up ahead.

"Great," Charlie said, sighing. "The path splits here. Which way?"

"I'll go with whatever you think, given your army experiences," Will said.

Charlie looked down at his phone. He was scrambling through the GPS maps. "I think Brimley's place must be this way," he said, picking the right path. "I really hope this one is our killer."

"That's a poor choice of words," Will said. "I'd rather he not be *our* killer, but rather *the* killer."

"You love to correct people, don't you Will?"

"I do have to say it's a weakness of mine. Call it a hobby."

The two men walked to the end of the path where it finally came to a large clearing. A wooden cottage sat peacefully in the middle of it, lonely and picturesque in the forest setting.

Charlie still thought a place with no car access was weird, and he worried that if he called for backup the cops would have difficulty finding the place in time.

It felt like another world away from the hustle and bustle of a normal, daily experience. But then, when you had been living in psychiatric wards for years like Robert Brimley had, maybe you needed to be away from society as much as possible.

As they approached, Charlie turned to Will: "Let's try and keep this as relaxed as possible. It feels like every potential perp I run across at the moment, I'm quickly greeted with a fist to the face."

Will nodded. He touched the bruising on his own face. "I feel that myself."

They walked up the wooden steps to a large porch and then knocked on the door of the cottage.

"Coming," the voice of an older woman said quickly. Light footsteps sounded and then stopped behind the door. "Who's there, please?"

"Marjorie, don't open that door!" Another gravelly voice sounded. This time a man.

Charlie looked at Will and raised an eyebrow in surprise.

"My name is Agent Carlson," he said. "I'm with the FBI. We are looking to speak with a Mr. Robert Brimley, if you don't mind."

"Dear sweet little Robert," the elderly woman's voice said. She started to undo a series of locks, and the elderly gentleman continued with his protests about opening the door.

"Calm down, Harold," she said. "It's the FBI."

"Ask to see some ID first before you take off the security chain." Harold was being cautious. It appeared that the house was home to an elderly couple, and Charlie didn't blame Harold for being a little hesitant living in the woods.

Charlie held up his ID to the door. The door opened slightly, the security chain still clinging on across the small gap. An elderly woman with a kind face peeked out. She looked at the badge and studied it for a moment.

She smiled and then undid the security chain.

The door opened fully revealing the old lady in a white cotton dress and shawl, with a man standing with a walking stick behind her, glaring over her shoulder. They both looked to be in their eighties at least.

"Is Robert with you, Ma'am?" Charlie asked.

"I'm afraid not," she said with a sad face. "He's not been with us for the last couple of weeks. He is my younger sister's boy you know. I said we'd take him in as she's not keeping well. Harold wasn't keen… Not after Robert had spent all that time in that nasty Wendel Institute."

"There must have been a reason he was there," Harold said grumpily. "They would have let him out sooner otherwise. Never keen on him anyway."

"Hush, Harold," Marjorie said. "Don't you speak bad of him in front of these nice men. Robert is a sweet soul and you know that."

"Where is he now, if you don't mind?" Will asked.

"He's in another psychiatric hospital on the other side of the country. He found a good one that could help him."

Harold moved forward behind Marjorie. "And a good thing too! The boy's head is full of broken glass. If you ask me, all this mental illness stuff, they just need a good kick up the you know what."

Charlie tried not to rise to that. The old man was clearly ignorant that most people suffered from mental health issues at some point in their lives. The old man probably had himself, though he'd most likely not want to admit it.

"That's not kind," Marjorie gave her husband a stare that would have turned a glass of water to ice. She then turned back to Will and Charlie. "Robert thought that the Wendel Institute had released him too soon and that he needed to continue treatment. He didn't feel right being out. So he traveled to California, to a new psychiatric hospital. Orchid Bay is the name of it. He writes us letters from there; he's doing well, but he isn't ready to come out. I can give you the number of the place if you would like?"

"That would be great, thank you," Charlie said. But his heart sank. He had the feeling now that Robert Brimley was yet another name they'd have to cross from their suspects list.

The old lady puttered around somewhere out of sight. The sound of something being knocked over came. Harold grumbled about it inside until Marjorie reappeared with a card.

She handed it to Charlie.

"That's his doctor's card," she said. "He's very good when talking about sweet Robert."

"Thank you for this," Charlie said. "How long has he been there?"

"At least two weeks... I think," Marjorie explained. "We're both retired my husband and I, the days kind of blend in together. It could be longer."

"Tell me about it," Charlie said. "Thank you for your time. You both have a great day."

"And you," Marjorie said, her husband grumbling away behind her about a draft of air coming through the hallway.

Charlie and Will walked away from the house back down the country path.

"That was a wasted journey," Charlie grimaced under his breath.

"Scientifically speaking," Will replied, "if that therapy center says Robert Brimley's been there for a couple of weeks, we've at least eliminated a possibility. That still a positive result, when you look at it from that perspective."

125

"I love your optimism, Will, but there's one thing you've forgotten."

"What's that?"

"If we've narrowed our suspects down to these last two men and it's not Robert Brimley…"

Will gasped.

"Then Valerie could be about to face the killer by herself!"

The two men didn't need to say anything else to each other. They started to run, tracing the path back through the forest. Charlie felt a fear he rarely experienced on the job. The fear that his partner, his friend, might be about to face death.

CHAPTER THIRTY

Valerie was happy her next suspect was taking her further out from Indianapolis. This stopped her from feeling guilty about not returning to see Tom's family.

The further she was away from that situation, the better it was for her guilt. Out of sight, out of mind. At least partially.

She wished she could have said the same for Jackson's call about her father's disappearance.

At least the last few miles of the drive had helped calm her, the sun streaming down, kissing the road surface with golden yellow. For moments, she almost forgot herself and her pain. As though she could melt into the summer scene like a painting and live forever in a happy place far removed from her weary mind.

She pulled up at the end of a small cul-de-sac and put the car into park.

Straight ahead, there was number 86. That was the last known address of one Michael Wainwright, former patient of Wendel Institute, and one of only two people on that list who lived in the area where the killer seemed to be moving through. Valerie wondered how Will and Charlie had gotten on with the other suspect.

She looked at her phone once more as if to double check everything she had put together so far. There were two missed calls from Charlie.

The signal must have been bad on part of that road, she thought, because she hadn't heard her phone. Although she couldn't discount that she had been numb from Jackson's call and blocked it out.

A text message from Will said that their suspect wasn't the killer and that she should be careful.

Valerie didn't reply. She was fed up with them fussing over her.

She swiped onto another app and saw the map of the killings on the screen. Michael Wainwright's house was at the end of the line of victims. Like a terminal where death was sure to show its face.

Valerie checked her revolver, steadied herself, and then left the car.

As she walked towards the detached house, she was amazed by how quiet the area was. Rushing from place to place chasing down fugitives most of her time, she had forgotten how the suburbs could have an unusual calm to them.

She wandered up through the well-kept front yard, and up to the front door of the property. She couldn't see anything out of the ordinary. If anything, the place was the epitome of everything normal in the world. But Valerie knew that some of humanity's most dangerous elements hid in such places, wrapping themselves up and passing themselves off as normal, protected by a warm womb of banality.

Raising her fist to knock on the door, it pulled open before she had the chance.

There in the sunlight, Valerie found herself face-to-face with a man at least 6' 3" tall, broad shouldered like a mountain, and with an intensity to his demeanor.

The man looked at Valerie for the briefest of seconds and then laughed as if he were shocked by her presence. "My word. You nearly scared me to death."

Valerie smiled, but deep down she would not drop her guard. She felt intimidated by the man's physicality, something which was unusual as that rarely happened to her.

Yet she was in a fragile place emotionally, and so the unusual was quickly becoming the norm.

"Sorry about that," Valerie said, trying to remain affable at least on the outside. Looking at the size of the man's arms alone, she thought *this is someone who could tear a person to pieces with their bare hands.*

"Can I be of some help to you?" the man said smiling.

But Valerie wasn't feeling his friendly vibe, she felt there was something underneath. Something serious and grim. She knew the look of someone trying to hold themselves together. She'd seen that look on her sister's face. On her mother's face. Even on her own from time to time.

And the man wore the same false expression.

"As a matter of fact, you may be able to help me," Valerie said, trying to keep the conversation going. "I'm Agent Law with the FBI.

She showed her ID.

Valerie noticed something change in the man's eyes as he stared at the badge. He was still smiling, but his eyes seemed dark and fierce, like Valerie's ID somehow enraged him. But if this was the case, he still managed to hold it together.

"You don't know a man named Michael Wainwright by any chance, do you?" Valerie asked.

"I should hope so," he said laughing a little too much. "I stare at his face in the mirror every morning. And let me tell you, it isn't a pretty sight."

He joked, but Valerie sensed deep down that he was being serious about that. The self-loathing was clear.

"Nice to meet you," Valerie offered. "We're investigating a series of murders in the area…"

"I read about that," he said. "Nasty stuff."

"It is," Valerie responded. "We believe that someone who has been recently released from the Wendel Institute after it closed might be responsible.

"And you think it's me?" Michael said, for the first time dropping the smile and harmless act.

"I never said that," Valerie explained. "But we are speaking with you and a number of others to see if anyone from the institute might know someone *they* think is the killer."

"Okay, okay," he said. "Sorry I don't like to talk about Wendel stuff."

Michael looked around as if to see if anyone was listening.

"My neighbors are real gossips," he whispered. "And they'd spread bad rumors around about me in a heartbeat."

Valerie now wondered if this was part of the man's paranoia coming through.

"I understand, but I really do need to talk with you about this."

He looked around again and then sighed. "Okay, but inside, away from prying ears."

Michael stepped back into his house and waited for Valerie to join him. But she hesitated for a moment when he motioned to her.

For the first time, she wished she hadn't been alone and that she'd had some backup. Something inside of her said *get out of here*, but she didn't listen to it. She couldn't. If she ran any time she felt fear, she wouldn't have been an FBI agent.

"Please, come in," Michael said, motioning from the hallway again.

Ignoring the warning in her heart, Valerie stepped over the threshold and disappeared inside the house. The sunlight of the outside world was quickly gone, replaced by the interior of the house, dim from most of the blinds being down.

"On your left, please," Michael said standing and pointing to an open doorway.

Valerie followed his directions and found herself in a quiet living room. But she was surprised at the blandness of it all. Like the yard outside, it was pristine. But everything in the room was either black in color or white.

The monotonal design raised alarm bells in Valerie's mind immediately.

"Can I get you a coffee?" Michael asked Valerie.

"No thank you," Valerie said sitting on a black leather couch.

She hoped he would sit down and appear more relaxed. But he did not.

"As I said outside, the case I'm investigating involves a number of recent murders," Valerie explained. "They've all taken place in and around Indianapolis."

"Yes, I read about some of this. It's terrible," the man said. But Valerie wasn't convinced that he meant it.

"We're speaking with every patient released from the Wendel Institute. It's just a few procedural questions and to see if you have any idea about other patients who were released, perhaps too soon?" Valerie said this, hoping she could make the man feel more at ease, and so he'd be more likely to slip up.

"There are plenty of people who came out of that place that could have done it," Michael said pointedly. "But I don't have any name particularly in my head, and I never really made friends there, so I don't stay in touch with anyone from there. I'd rather leave all of that behind anyway. If you ask me, that place made people violent rather than helping them." When Michael said this, his expression changed as he clenched his teeth. Then, he smiled, like an actor suddenly remembering the part he was playing for the audience.

"Did you ever come into contact with anyone from Ward 17 specifically?" Valerie asked. "I hear some of the most difficult patients were treated there, and that their therapy protocols were borderline abusive."

Michael shook his head for a moment in disbelief, as if Valerie had uttered and brought up something painful.

"It was more than abuse," he seethed. "They experimented on us with their medications and electric shock therapy."

"You weren't put in there, were you Mr. Wainwright?" Valerie asked. "Feel free to talk about it, it might help us."

"I *hated* that place," he said. "I don't want to talk about it, but I can at least tell you that anyone who went into that ward, never quite came out the same."

"So, what type…"

"I won't answer any more questions about that place," he said, cutting her off.

Valerie didn't want to lose him by pressing too hard. She would come back to the institute. For now, she'd change tactics. She needed to rule him out from her investigation.

"If you don't mind," Valerie said. "Can you tell me your whereabouts of the last few days?"

He was stone-faced for a moment. "I'm afraid with my condition, Agent…"

"Law," Valerie answered.

"I'm afraid with my specific condition, I have issues with my memory. But I can go and get my diary, and then we can go through all of your dates one by one, if that's okay?"

"Of course," Valerie said. She felt a suspicion about this. Someone with memory problems would have fit the profile, especially if their long term memory was intact. That way, he would be functional enough to evade capture, but disorientated in spells, perhaps leading to a violent outburst.

Michael Wainwright, still towering above Valerie, walked through the doorway and could be heard going into a nearby room.

"Hold on a second," he said loudly from somewhere through the wall.

"No problem," Valerie said.

She looked around again in the room.

Then it made sense to her. The blankness of the room. Everything was in black or white. This made Valerie feel like Wainwright was suffering from some sort of issue with over stimulation. Perhaps keeping everything muted stopped him from being triggered psychologically. Valerie knew that such conditions could lead to emotional regulation and impulse control issues when over stimulated.

That was a fit for the profile she and her team were working on. And the memory issues could have been the mechanism fueling such loss of control.

Just as that thought occurred to Valerie, Michael reappeared with a large diary in his hand. He stepped towards Valerie and then sat down next to her. She felt the couch slump under his size.

"Everything you need is in here," he said.

131

Valerie only saw the glint of the metal at the last moment. Michael then opened the diary and grabbed at a knife concealed between its pages. He thrust it towards Valerie, and only at the last moment did she manage to fling herself off the couch. And onto the floor.

The knife swished by her and cut into the couch.

Valerie scrambled for the door, pulling out her gun. She put her finger on the trigger as Michael Wainwright rushed towards her. Valerie turned and then let off a shot.

It struck her attacker in the shoulder.

He let out an agonizing scream, but he did not stop moving forward. Valerie squeezed the trigger again, but now the hulking figure was upon her, arms reaching. He grasped at the gun and wrenched it from her hand. Her finger caught in the trigger and the gun went off again, the bullet splintering in the wall behind them.

Valerie struck upwards, catching the man on the chin, but it felt like she was hitting granite.

He put his hands around her throat; she felt the oxygen quickly being halted to her brain.

She knew she had only moments before she passed out, and then Wainwright could do what he wanted with her. Valerie stuck her hand forward with force, and prodded her thumb into the man's eye. He yelped like an animal and reached up instinctively to stop her.

That gave Valerie a chance.

She pivoted and was able to crawl out from underneath the man's huge frame. She scrambled to the door, with Michael Wainwright straight onto her, unstoppable.

He grabbed her hair and yanked backwards just as she thought she was escaping.

Valerie wailed in pain.

She dragged her foot down the man's shin and then kept punching at his face and body. But he was too strong, too resilient. Ward 17 had given him that.

Valerie felt a cold shiver work its way up through her body as he grabbed her again. She was facing death head on, and death was winning.

The man wrapped his hand around her face and thrust her into a wall. He readied his fist to strike, but suddenly two sets of hands reached around and grabbed him by the neck and arms.

He fell back.

Valerie felt blood trickle from the back of her head. She felt dazed and fell onto one knee. When she looked up, she stayed conscious long enough to see her two partners wrestling with the man. Will was thrust to the side, and Michael Wainwright gripped his knife and jabbed it towards Will's chest in rage.

Charlie had no option to save his friend. He fired twice, each one hitting its mark. Michael Wainwright finally collapsed, writhing in agony, and Valerie closed her eyes, losing consciousness.

CHAPTER THIRTY ONE

He didn't want to kill again, but he would do it each time that woman showed her face to him. Each time she hunted him down, he would have to snuff her out like a candle.

But he was growing tired of the constant running. He needed to rest, and he had long been heading to that one place of safety.

He knew his only hope of respite, no matter how brief, was to find somewhere, a sanctuary. A place where *the woman* could not find him and could not taunt him with her existence.

At the very least, a place where she would be powerless to enter.

Sanctuary could only come from one place: Home. The place where his mother had raised him and he had spent all of his life.

At first, he had done everything he could to avoid going home. He didn't want to be there, not after his mother had died back at the hospital. But those days of wandering, of running from the woman who was terrorizing him, that had made him realize there was only one safe place, and it would be safe for a reason.

His delusions had told him that his mother would protect him, even from beyond the grave.

Turning a corner he'd walked a hundred thousand times since he was a child, he saw his home come into view. The house where he had left his entire life behind just a few days previously when his mother had died.

The house sat alongside many others, but the killer knew it was special. In front of it was the yard where he'd played ball with his dad before he died. The garage where he'd worked on his first car. And the door... The door where he felt sanctuary waited for him on the other side.

He looked around the empty street. He wanted to make sure that the woman wasn't watching. He worried that she was hiding somewhere nearby, waiting for him.

She mustn't know where I live, he thought.

That would have been a disaster.

Though the man believed that the house would be protected by his mother's energy in death, if the woman found him, she would find other ways to torture him. He imagined seeing that face waiting in the street, ensuring that he would become a prisoner in his home by never daring to leave and face her.

For a moment, the face flashed in his mind. He hallucinated it hovering up at his bedroom window on the first floor, pressing against the glass and grinning wide.

He shook the image from his mind.

Once he was happy that he was truly on his own, he crossed the road, took out the keys in his pocket, quickly entered, closing the door behind him.

The house smelled different. It felt different. He took a deep breath.

How much of his mother lingered there?

He hadn't believed in ghosts, not until a few weeks ago. But since then he had been haunted by a specter of death. If *she* could come back to terrorize him, why couldn't his mother come back from death to help?

His mom had done everything for him in life. If there was a way for the dead to come back, she would find it; she would protect him.

A few weeks ago, his mother had died back at the hospital. It was a stroke, they'd said. Like the most nonchalant thing in the world. An everyday occurrence.

How could the hospital staff not see that one of the world's greatest people had just died?

He had done everything to protect her. Countless weeks and months at the hospital, sitting next to her bed and holding her hand. But in the end his love wasn't enough to keep her alive. She succumbed to the illness. And something broke inside of him.

Suddenly, from behind him, a knock came at the door.

He couldn't believe it. Had the woman found him so quickly already? Was it possible?

He reasoned that the dead could do what they like.

Staring at the door, he imagined her on the other side grinning, waiting to torture him once more.

He begged for someone to rescue him from her.

"Mom? Please help me...," he said to the empty house.

But it was indeed empty. Empty of the love his mother once gave him. Empty of her life. She was dead. He was alone.

The grief washed over him, and it was quickly joined by anger. Anger that the world had taken his mother from him. That it had robbed him of the only person who understood him. The only one to look after him.

And all because of the other woman and what she did!

The anger swelled inside of him like a burning pit of hate. He clenched his fists, grabbed the handle, and swung the door open.

There she was. With him again. The same woman as always. Oh, she was disguised this time as some door-to-door charity worker, but he knew better. It was her. The eyes were the giveaway.

He almost spat in her face.

"Hello, I was wondering if you had a few moments to talk about our charity?" the woman said, grinning.

Then a thought occurred to the man. Another delusional, disconnected thought.

She's made a mistake.

In his paranoid mind, he felt that if he killed the woman inside his family home where his mother had spent most of her days, that would be enough. That would dispel the woman's negative energy and stop her from manifesting ever again.

With rage and delight in equal measure, he reached out and grabbed the woman by the arm and then yanked her inside slamming the door.

She screamed.

It was pitiful to him.

"Don't hurt me!" she cried.

"The you shouldn't have hurt my family!" he cried out.

She spoke of wanting mercy. But what mercy had she given him or his mother?

None.

And he would show her the same.

He struck her across the face and she reeled backwards onto the floor. Rushing over, he raised his foot and struck her in the face.

I'll crush that grinning face once and for all, he thought.

But as he kicked out a second time, the woman rolled out of the way and was able to scramble up onto her feet. He quickly pulled out the knife in his pocket, the same knife, in his mind, he'd used to kill her several times already.

He jabbed with it and caught her in the arm. Blood spurted out onto him. The idea of her blood sullying his mother's home enraged him even more.

She screamed.

He stabbed again catching her in the side. He felt the blade go in a couple of inches just underneath her ribs.

She let out a horrible gasp. He was glad that she was suffering.

But then she took him by surprise. Though she was reeling from the attack, she suddenly rallied and struck out with her hands, scratching down his left eye.

The pain was blinding. And when he brushed the blood away from his face, he watched in horror as she quickly made her way to the front door, opened it, and ran screaming over the threshold.

Reaching out, the killer yanked her hair back and slammed her onto the floor.

He would kill her, but now it wasn't safe to linger. The neighbors would have heard that scream. They would call the police.

The killer searched his brain. He needed to be somewhere safe. Somewhere no one could harm him.

His mind moved back in time to when he was a child, and the place was chosen. In his twisted mind, it would provide him sanctuary, from the police, from *her*.

And then the thought entered his mind like a flash of brilliance. *Bring her with you,* the thought said. If he brought her to such a sacred place and spilled her blood on its grounds, surely his curse would be lifted and he would be left alone in peace?

He pulled the woman to her feet and searched for his car keys. They were going on a drive, and he fully intended that his hostage would never return alive from it.

CHAPTER THIRTY TWO

Valerie smelled something horrible, like a mix of sulfur and dead fish. She opened her eyes at the smell of it, coming out of a deep, dark sleep.

She gasped loudly as a paramedic sat over her. She looked around and saw that she was in the back of an ambulance. Charlie and Will sat alongside her.

"You're going to be okay," the paramedic said. "You've not been completely out of it, just dazed. I had to bring you round with smelling salts, though."

Valerie nodded. She sat up slowly.

"Are you okay?" Charlie asked.

"Yeah," Valerie said.

"You'll need to be checked out by a doctor at the hospital," the paramedic said.

"I'm fine. Honestly."

Valerie saw Charlie and Will give a glance to each other.

"You're the expert at catching psychopathic criminals, Valerie," Will said gently. "But maybe we should listen to the medical experts when it comes to passing out?"

Valerie sighed. She knew he was right, but she was eager to get going.

"We caught him, though," she said, smiling. "We got him!"

Charlie looked at Valerie with a solemn expression.

"What? What is it?" Valerie asked, her heart sinking.

"Michael Wainwright isn't the killer, Val," Charlie said. And suddenly the world was a lot more dangerous again.

*

The bright lights of the hospital corridor hurt Valerie's eyes. She was mortified about the situation.

Charlie pushed the wheelchair she was sitting in, and Will walked alongside.

"This is ridiculous," Valerie said under her breath.

"Just let us get you seen by a doctor, Val," Charlie said.

"I can walk perfectly fine," Valerie stated, exasperated.

"Valerie," Will said, gently. "You seemed a bit woozy from the impact on your head fighting Michael Wainwright You lost consciousness for a moment. You can't mess around with a head injury like that. Let's get you checked out before you go rushing after the next suspect."

Charlie stopped pushing, bringing Valerie to a stop. They were standing at a cross section of corridors. The bland fluorescent lighting made it look almost exactly the same as every other corridor they had been through already.

"Ugh," Charlie said.

"Are you lost, Charlie?" Valerie said. "Maybe I should be pushing you around."

"It's kind of like coming full circle being here," Will said. "The same hospital where the first victim was killed. Well, in the parking lot. And here we are, again."

"I know," Valerie said gravely. It didn't feel right her being there as a patient. It felt like a cruel defeat, to be sent to the place where the first victim worked. And all because she had ended up down another dead end.

"Which way?" Charlie seemed to be talking to himself. "They all look the same."

"I think I saw a sign back there for the triage," Valerie pointed out. "Turn right here."

As Charlie pushed Valerie along the corridor, a torrent of thoughts swirled in her head. Something was ruminating in her subconscious. But she couldn't be sure what.

The only thing she was certain of, was that being back at the hospital was the cause. She felt like she was staring at one of those magic eye pictures, knowing that something is there and just waiting for her brain to reveal it.

"Are we sure Michael Wainwright isn't the killer?" Valerie asked.

"Positive," Charlie said. "He's not, but he would have killed you. Apparently he was sectioned for a few nights and spent 8 days in a different psychiatric hospital recently. Two of the murders were committed in that time, so it can't be him. But make no mistake, he would have killed you... I can't believe he's still alive, either. I shot him point blank. The man is a mountain."

139

Charlie turned another corner, then continued talking.

"I do wonder why he tried to kill you with that knife?" he mused. "Why was Wainwright intent on killing you if he had nothing to do with the murders? I'm just glad he's in custody now."

"His home explains it," Valerie said. "He controlled every aspect of that place, right down to the strange monotonal decor. He no doubt had a severe impulse control issue. Just bad luck for me that his impulses were violent. I would like to know more about his past, though."

"I can help with that," said Will. "He was definitely someone with impulse control issues. Remember that colleague I had that worked at the Wendel Institute? I put a call in. They said they believe he was put into Ward 17. And that seems to have made him worse."

Valerie slammed her closed fist on the arm of the wheelchair. "How many people did those bastards ruin?"

"Again," said Will. "It's a chicken and the egg scenario. Ward 17 was where the most violent and dangerous patients were treated. But were they truly violent before they went in or after?"

"We'll probably never know the answer," Valerie said. "Hopefully there'll be a public inquiry One thing is certain, whatever they were trying in that ward, the medications, surgery, electric shock therapy: It certainly didn't help them."

"Do you want some more good news?" Charlie asked.

Valerie sighed. "No."

"I heard from Quantico while the ambulance brought you here, Val," he said. "Between local law enforcement and other agents, we've exhausted the possibilities. Everyone has checked out with an alibi or as an unlikely suspect."

"Then after all of this," Will said. "All the violence. All the death. We're right back to square one, with no theory about who this killer is."

Valerie knew Will was right. With all their detective work and insights, they were now at a dead end. Valerie wondered if the killer was about to go dark, and the case would remain unsolved forever.

CHAPTER THIRTY THREE

Charlie pushed Val's chair into a small waiting room, and Valerie hated every minute of it.

"I'm agent Carlson," Charlie said to an approaching nurse. "We called ahead?"

"Yes," the nurse smiled. "This way please."

Charlie pushed and Will followed. They were escorted by the nurse through a set of double doors and then into an assessment room.

Valerie wasn't looking forward to being poked and prodded by a doctor. She wasn't feeling woozy anymore from the cut on the back of her head, but Will and Charlie were fussing like two mother hens.

A doctor soon entered the room, short with glasses and a bright bow tie. Valerie could tell he was kind of quirky, but he seemed harmless enough.

"Hello Agent Law, I'm Doctor Reagan." They shook hands, and he looked over some notes he had on a tablet.

"I'm feeling fine, Doctor," Valerie maintained.

"It says here there paramedics patched up the wound on your head. Have you been feeling nauseous at all?"

"No."

"Off balance?"

"No.

"Overly sensitive to light?"

"Not really. Not any more than usual."

"Any headaches?"

"Yes. A six-foot-three-inch maniac smashed the back of my head off a wall."

The doctor took out a light and shone it in Valerie's eyes. He asked her to follow the light and then switched it off.

"Okay," he said. "I don't see anything overly concerning. Take some painkillers for your head, and if you start to vomit or feel faint, I want you back in here, agreed?"

"Thanks, Doctor."

He turned to leave and then stopped.

"Is something the matter, Doctor Reagan?" Will asked.

The doctor turned around to face them.

"We don't often get FBI agents in here," he said, hesitating. "You're not looking for this maniac who has been killing women in the area are you?"

Valerie felt herself tense up for a moment. She was in no mood to go over the case. But then she remembered. This was the same hospital where the first victim had worked. And she had been killed in the parking lot out back.

"Yeah," Valerie said. "We are… You didn't know the first victim, did you?"

The doctor nodded and looked visibly upset.

Will pulled out a chair and brought it over to him. "Please, Doctor, why don't you sit for a moment? We'd be happy to answer any questions you have."

The doctor nodded and sat down. He suddenly had the look of someone who had been working for many hours straight without a break.

He rubbed his forehead.

"I knew Maria Johansson," Doctor Reagan said softly. "A lovely person. The best nurse I ever saw, and I don't say that as some meaningless platitude because she's dead. I really mean it."

"I know you do," Valerie said. She could see Charlie looking at her. It was as if they both felt it. Almost like the hand of fate guiding them. Bringing them, as Will had put it, full circle to the scene of the first murder. And now to be sitting with someone who clearly cared deeply about the victim.

"She was so good with end of life care," the doctor said. "She went the extra mile. She sat with many patients who had no one as they died. And if the family was there, she was always willing to give them a shoulder to cry on."

"She sounds wonderful," Charlie offered.

"She was… I don't understand how someone could have done that to her," the doctor said almost to no one. "Who would kill such a sweet soul? Who could be that filled with hate to randomly murder a nurse?"

Something jolted in Valerie's mind. She stood up out of the wheelchair quickly.

"What's wrong, Val?" Charlie asked.

"Hold on…" She tried to think through it. She paced up and down on the spot until the theory clicked into place and she was ready to

142

reveal it.

"We know the killer is murdering these women because they look alike," Valerie said. "But what if that isn't *exactly* right. What if we've got it upside down?"

"How do you mean?" asked Will.

"Remember my theory, that he was someone who had never killed before. That he'd never been in an institute. That he wasn't on the Wendel list?"

"Yes," said Charlie. "It seems more likely now that we've exhausted the list."

"Agreed," Will interjected.

"I theorized a few days ago the possibility," Valerie continued, "that this killer didn't fit the usual serial killer profile. He wouldn't have had the same red flags. There would have been no escalation from abuse to killing animals, to hunting people."

"Instead, there would have been a catalyst moment. Something happened that made him break. And after that? He started murdering the women who looked similar to each other."

"I still don't see where you're going with this?" Will observed.

"What if it isn't that the victims all look alike. But rather, that they all look like the killer's *first* victim. What if Maria Johansson was the first target? Then he keeps killing her over and over again. And why? Because she is deeply connected to the event that caused the killer to have his mental break! A death in the family right here in this hospital!"

Valerie felt exhilarated. For the first time on this case, she felt like the fog had cleared. She was no longer encumbered by her personal problems. She was thinking at the top of her game.

In her elated mood, she wondered if her near death experience with Michael Wainwright had jolted her out of her funk.

"It's as good a theory as any other we might have," Will said. He turned to the doctor who was still sitting down. "Doctor Reagan, you said Maria was excellent at comforting families in the wake of a death. Do you know if there was any issue with a family member of a patient before Maria was murdered?"

"Actually," he said. "There was, come to think of it. Hal Borchardt. I remember him. He'd been so dedicated to his mother, always visiting. But when his mother died, he blamed the staff. Maria was the nurse who had been assigned to the mother that day... My God... Could he be the killer?"

"Did you mention this to the police when you were interviewed?" Valerie asked.

"No," the doctor replied. "I didn't think about it until you mentioned it. We deal with families all the time at their most trying moments. It's not unusual for someone to question the nurses and doctors about the care they're giving. It's pretty common for someone to get angry at us. We try not to take it personally."

"Doctor," Charlie stepped forward. "We're going to need Hal Borchardt's mother's details, and his, if you have them on record. And I don't want to hear about hospital confidentiality. This guy might have been the one who killed your colleague."

"You won't hear a complaint from me," he said, standing up. "Just give me a moment, I'll need to make a call."

He left the room.

Will, Valerie, and Charlie all looked at each other.

"I can feel it in my bones," Valerie said. "Hal Borchardt is the killer. I know it. It all makes sense. Now we need to find him."

Valerie just hoped that the hospital had his last known address.

CHAPTER THIRTY FOUR

Valerie was frustrated when she saw several patrol cars sitting on the street corner as the sun began to set in the distance.

"God dammit," Valerie said to Charlie from the passenger seat. "We told local PD to keep a low profile. Only go in if they had to."

Several people, most likely neighbors, were out talking with the cops. Faces etched in worry.

"If Hal Borchardt didn't know we were coming," Will said from the back seat, "he will now."

Charlie parked the car and the three investigators got out.

Valerie walked up to one of the patrol cars, but she didn't have the time to be dressing down one of the officers for being overzealous, even if they did deserve it. The mistake had already been made.

"Is there any evidence someone's inside?" she asked.

One of the officers shook his head. "No, Agent Law. No sign."

Valerie peered across the road to the house. It was like any other at first glance. And yet unlike any other. It played host to a violent killer, if Valerie's theory was correct.

It was the home of Hal Borchardt and his deceased mother, Miriam.

"Will, you stay here for now, okay?" Valerie said. "Charlie and I will go in."

Will nodded, though Valerie could see that he felt conflicted about not being able to assist more directly. Valerie trusted him implicitly, but he was still an academic, and she and Charlie were trained agents.

Valerie checked her gun in her holster, and watched Charlie as he did the same with his.

"You ready?" Charlie asked.

"Let's do this," Valerie said. She was part exhilarated, feeling mentally at the top of her game for the first time in weeks. But there was still apprehension. She felt it in the very fabric of her being; she was about to enter the home of the killer they had been chasing all this time.

They walked across the street together, their guns still resting in their holsters. After all, Hal Borchardt was only a suspect. They didn't want to go barging in and waving guns in his face. It was that type of overzealous behavior, that got many an agent into trouble. When on a case for some time, agents had to be careful when the endgame came. It was too easy to get carried away and make a fatal mistake, running straight into the barrel of a gun when so close to an arrest.

They walked up the path in the yard and came to the door. Valerie kept her eyes trained on the windows, looking for any sign of life. There was none. This was a place life had long since abandoned.

Valerie then saw something.

She looked down at the bottom of the closed front door. There was a streak of blood across it.

"Charlie?" she said, pointing to it.

"I'd say that gives us probable cause," he said, drawing his weapon.

Valerie agreed. She drew her gun and nodded to Charlie to give him the go ahead for entry.

Charlie stepped back and then thrust his foot against the door, it was old and relented immediately. The lock splintered, and Charlie rushed straight in. Valerie was close behind.

"FBI, Hal Borchardt, come out with your hands up!" Charlie shouted.

They waited in the lobby of the house. All they could hear was a creak occasionally sounding somewhere. Nothing else moved.

Valerie looked down and saw more blood inside. It looked like someone had lost a decent amount.

Her heart sank. Had he claimed another victim?

Valerie swept each room slowly, methodically, but each room came up empty. Once they headed up the stairs to the top floor, Valerie moved with more apprehension.

The lights were off and the blinds were down. With the sun setting outside, it was a dark affair. The corners were pockets of shadows that seemed to stare at Valerie as she passed.

She half imagined a pair of arms appearing from the corner of each room, and then grabbing her and pulling her into a warm, rotten embrace.

There was one room left, and Valerie hoped that it would contain the still living body of Hal's current target.

Valerie decided to go in first this time. She stood with Charlie to the rear and pushed the door open, her revolver held tightly in her hand, stretched out in front of her.

The room was Hal Borchardt's mother's. When Valerie had gotten her details from the hospital, she'd discovered that her name was Miriam.

It looked like she was religious. A set of rosary beads sat on a small dresser, at the foot of a mirror. The room was cozy, but not too large or filled with junk. It was simple.

Valerie caught a faint whiff of the old lady's perfume. She wondered for a moment if anything else of people lingers beyond their possessions after death.

She lowered her gun.

"He's not here," Valerie said, disappointed.

"Whose blood is that downstairs?" Charlie asked.

"Either another victim or he's been hurt, maybe during a recent attack."

"It's nighttime," Charlie said. "The blood is fresh; he's definitely been here. But why isn't here right now? Shouldn't he be going to bed if he's in the vicinity?"

"That makes me think the blood is from a victim," Valerie thought out loud.

"But who?"

Valerie thought it through for a moment. "It must have been someone who randomly came by, like a door-to-door salesman. I doubt it was a neighbor."

"Why?" Charlie said.

"Well, I've been giving it some thought. The killer only murders when someone crosses his path and they look vaguely like Maria Johansson, the nurse. I think he's just like Michael Wainwright He has an impulsive streak. It's never planned. If Hal has attacked someone on his own doorstep, it's because they were here uninvited."

Valerie paced in the room for a second and scratched her cheek as she tried to put it together.

"Remember the jogger he murdered?" she asked Charlie.

"Yeah."

"When she phoned 911, he was on the ground writhing about," Valerie said. "He's clearly deranged. I think he's most likely murdering the victims, not just because he thinks they look like Maria Johansson, but because his delusion runs so deep, that he thinks they *are* Maria Johansson. That would explain the impulsivity of it."

"That's why he's not going out and seeking these people like a true serial killer does, hunting. It can't have been a neighbor who knocked on the door, because he would have known who they were *and* that

147

they weren't the nurse. It always has to be a stranger and he convinces himself he has to kill them again because the nurse represents the death of his mother, and he wants to erase that from the world!"

"So you think this guy isn't culpable for his actions?" Charlie asked.

"Possibly," Valerie said. "Right now, regardless, he's lethally dangerous. We need to put out an APB through the local PD for Hal Borchardt. He's armed, dangerous, and he may even have a hostage with him."

"A hostage?" Charlie said sounding surprised. "But he usually just kills."

"My hunch is, he attacked the woman at the door, then realized what he'd done. It was too dangerous to stay. He's either moved the body or she's alive and he's taking her somewhere to finish the job."

Charlie rushed downstairs to speak with the police officers on the street.

Valerie turned to the dresser next to Miriam Borchardt's bed. She picked up a small picture frame, popped out the photograph and put it in her pocket.

Maybe he'll talk with his mother, if it comes to it, Valerie thought to herself.

Then another thought occurred. Days ago, she'd theorized that the killer was off his meds, and that this was playing into his delusions.

Valerie walked into the bathroom on that level. She opened the bathroom cabinet and saw several packets of heavy anti-depressants and anti-psychotic medications. Going by the dates on them, Hal had indeed skipped his meds.

She shook her head. She almost felt sorry for him. Normally she couldn't sympathize with a killer. But Hal... If her theory was right, he wasn't really in control of his actions. He felt like he was being hounded, seeing the same face of the nurse over and over again.

But that didn't absolve him of what he'd done. Of how many families he'd destroyed with the flick of a knife.

Valerie moved out of the bathroom as Charlie came back into the house, this time with Will in tow.

"Charlie filled me in on everything," Will said. "It looks like Hal is the killer, but now we have to find where he is, and if his next victim is with him..."

"Agreed, but we don't have anything to go on, yet," Charlie said. "Unless... Could there be something here that would suggest where he might go?"

There was a silence for a moment as they mulled it over. "I think you might be onto something, Charlie," Will said. He looked deep in thought for a moment.

Valerie sensed he was thinking through an idea.

Will started to look around without saying anything.

"What are you looking for?" Valerie asked.

"Why did the killer come back here after roaming around all this time?" Will asked, clearly with an answer already in mind.

Valerie thought for a moment.

"Safety," Charlie said, thoughtfully. "When we're going through something stressful, we all pine for our home. Especially where we grew up, and it looks like Hal spent his entire life here."

"Yes," Valerie said. "It makes sense. He came home because he needed somewhere to feel safe. Then, a woman appears at his door, and he attacks her... He couldn't stay *here* anymore after that. But what if he took the woman to another place? Somewhere that he connected deeply with his past... Another place of refuge... Like he was trying to relive a happy memory connected with his mother."

"Which one is his room?" Will asked.

Charlie pointed to the third door on the right.

Will walked in and then reappeared almost immediately, but now he was holding a picture frame.

"He kept this by his bedside," Will said, showing it to Valerie.

Valerie looked at the photograph. It showed a boy, presumably Hal, standing with his mother and father. His hand was holding a large cotton candy. They were smiling.

Behind them was a fairground.

"Take it out of the frame," Valerie said. "There might be something written on the back."

Will did just that.

"You're right," he said, handing it to Valerie.

On the back of the photograph it read "the best day of my life."

Footsteps suddenly sounded on the staircase. It was one of the police officers from outside.

"Agent Law, one of the neighbors said he saw Hal driving away from here about an hour ago with a woman in the backseat."

Valerie turned to Charlie. "He's still got the woman with him."

"We don't have much time," Will said. "He could kill her at any moment, if he hasn't already."

Valerie looked down at the photograph again.

"The best day…" she said, trailing off before turning to the police officer with purpose. "Get me a list of every fairground in the area, now!"

CHAPTER THIRTY FIVE

Valerie held onto the dashboard as Charlie zipped through the traffic at speed. Will looked on from the backseat.

Through the windscreen a huge Ferris wheel glowed against the stark night sky as Charlie screeched the car to a halt at the gates of a bustling amusement park.

As Valerie opened the car door and leaped out, the lights and sounds of the amusement park pinged and whizzed. She could smell cotton candy in the air; it brought back memories of her mom and dad taking her and Suzie to such places when she was young.

Will stuck his head out of the rear passenger window. "I think I should come with you this time."

Valerie agreed. Time was of the essence. Hal Borchardt's car had been found parked not far from the amusement park. This wasn't the time to be timid. It was all hands on deck. A woman's life was at stake.

They were stopped by someone dressed as an old Victorian strong man at the turnstile. He was about to go into some spiel about the sights and sounds of the amusement park, but Valerie dispensed with this immediately and showed her badge.

"FBI," she said. "We believe a violent killer is loose inside your park."

The man's face drained of color.

"Oh no," he said, turning and looking over his shoulder at the crowds of people laughing and moving between the rides. "Should I shut it down?"

"Not yet," Valerie said. "We don't want to spook him into doing something."

"We'll handle this," Charlie said alongside Valerie. "If we need the park evacuated, we'll let you know."

Valerie, Will, and Charlie passed through the turnstile. She could smell the cotton candy now mixing with roasted peanuts and the unmistakable smell of hot dogs.

"Which way?" Charlie asked, looking through the crowds.

"We need to split up," Valerie said. "You and Will check out the east side of the park; I'll check the west."

"Will you be…" Will began asking.

"This is what I do, Will," Valerie said. "You be careful."

And then they split up. Charlie and Will headed towards some bumper cars and the Ferris wheel.

Valerie moved quickly to the west side of the park.

"Where are you, Hal Borchardt," she said to herself as she darted from ride to ride. She was looking for a man and a wounded woman. But it was impossible to see through the crowds.

Valerie had to stop for a moment. She had to think it through.

Where would he go?

People passed en masse. The rides pinged and sounded in a cacophony of delighted cheers and screams.

But Valerie closed her eyes. She became an island of serenity in that sea of excess. She breathed deeply, and put herself in place of Hal. A man who had lost his mother. A man who felt haunted by the face of the nurse who had looked after her.

The guilt.

The fear.

The paranoia.

She let it all in.

"You're just a boy, Hal," she said to herself. "You're a boy here in this amusement park. Just like you were when your mother and father brought you here all those years ago."

Valerie thought back to the photograph of him holding cotton candy, smiling with his mother and father. She remembered the ride whizzing past behind in the image.

What was it? she thought.

Opening her eyes, she looked around for something similar. Something with red paint. Something that moved so fast the camera had only collected it as a blur in the photograph.

She looked up.

"The roller coaster!" she said out loud. But her voice was drowned out by those having fun around her. Wide grinning faces, wide eyes in the night.

Valerie ran towards the roller coaster and saw it. A small stand where they were selling pink candy floss. It was just to the side of the red canopy, welcoming people onto the ride.

The crowds parted momentarily like the Red Sea, and Valerie spied the two of them. A woman who looked sheet white, wrapped in a long coat, most probably obscuring her wounds. Her head bobbed slightly, and she looked like she was struggling to stay conscious.

And a man sitting next to her on a bench. His arm was around her shoulders. He was eating cotton candy, and although Valerie couldn't see it, she was convinced he was holding a knife to the woman's side, keeping her there in place.

Valerie walked through the passing crowds like they were swaying trees in a gleeful forest.

The man looked up from the bench as he took a bite of his cotton candy.

His hair was a matted mess. He looked like he hadn't slept in many days. And his eyes… Valerie had seen that look before. It was the darting gaze of someone caught in the midst of a complete paranoid breakdown.

Valerie walked over to the two figures and noticed beneath where the woman was sitting, blood was dripping down from the seat. She was badly injured.

She looked up and saw Valerie. They locked eyes. Valerie nodded. And the woman's face, full of terror, flinched. She could clearly see someone had come to help her.

And that person was Agent Valerie Law.

Valerie didn't draw her weapon. One push of Hal's knife could kill the woman next to him. She was going to have to talk him down.

She stopped alongside the bench.

Hal looked up at her.

All Valerie could see was a frightened boy. But a frightened boy capable of the most violent murders.

"Hello Hal," Valerie said, loud enough for him to hear.

"You… You know me?" he said.

"I know you're afraid," Valerie said. "But I'm here to help you… Is that a knife you're digging into this woman's side?"

Hal nodded slowly. "She's got to die. She's got to stop following me!"

"I know," Valerie said. "I'm an expert in this sort of thing. I can make her stop following you, Hal. But first, you have to give me the knife, okay?"

"No!" he said, throwing the cotton candy to the ground. "She'll come back then!"

"She's not the nurse from the hospital, Hal," Valerie said. "She's an innocent person you just think is the nurse. It's because you haven't

153

been taking your meds. And what happened to your mom."

Hal stood up quickly, yanking the poor woman wrapped in the coat next to him onto her feet.

"You lie! The meds are to control me! They're all in on it. What they did to my mom... They killed her! And now they want to torture me!"

He swung with the knife and Valerie darted out of the way. But he swung with his other fist and caught her on the side of the head, dazing her.

People started screaming, seeing the killer finally among them.

Hal grabbed the woman and put the knife to her throat. His eyes darted crazily around him.

Valerie regained her composure.

"Hal, let me help you..."

"No! You're in on it. You're all in on it!"

He yanked the woman backwards and dragged her into the running crowds, up to the roller coaster canopy. He swung the knife at anyone in his way and dragged the girl onto one of the carts.

Valerie drew her gun and moved forward. But she couldn't get a clean shot.

"Turn this thing on or... Or she dies!" Hal screamed.

A frightened looking man at the roller coaster, flicked a switch and the carts started moving on the track.

Valerie only had seconds to react. She ran as fast as she could as the carts gathered speed, and she leapt onto the back one, smacking her side against the safety bar.

The roller coaster was now moving at speed as it climbed up and up on the track. There was no way Valerie could get a clear shot. But she *had* to save the girl one way or another.

She refused to look down as her heart raced, and she vaulted over one of the carts as it moved up and up towards the peak of a large drop.

"Hal! She's not the nurse!"

"I'll kill her!" Hal said.

As the coaster reached the top of the hill, preparing to drop down at insane speeds, Valerie watching in horror as Hal pushed the woman in the coat to the side.

Her body rattled off one of the sides of the cart.

Valerie reached out and grabbed her hand.

The woman dangled over a deathly drop.

Hal seethed and lunged forward with his knife.

All Valerie could do was kick out with her leg, catching him in the stomach. In that dazed moment, she pulled the woman into the cart.

"Hold on!" Valerie screamed as the cart careened down the track.

It dipped and swerved as the three passengers were knocked from side to side.

Valerie wrapped her arm around one of the safety bars as the momentum of the carts nearly flung her out onto the concrete below.

People screamed from down there, looking like tiny ants crying out at what was happening above.

The coaster reached a straight, and things stabilized momentarily.

Hal lunged forward with his knife at Valerie, but she caught his hand.

Hal tumbled on top of her.

Valerie had flashes of Michael Wainwright trying to choke the life from her.

She pushed the knife against the metal of the cart, and then dug her hand into her pocket. As Hal pulled the knife up ready to pierce Valerie's chest with it, Valerie pulled out the photograph of Hal's mother.

"What would your mother think of her son, the murderer?" she screamed.

Hal stopped. His eyes filled with tears, and his hand lowered for a moment.

Valerie wasn't taking any other chances, she leaped up and pinned him to the floor of the cart.

The coaster suddenly stopped and the jolted to a halt. Valerie looked up to see Will and Charlie standing to the side. She was safely on the ground, and Valerie had single handedly caught the killer before he could murder again.

EPILOGUE

Valerie smiled at Tom's dad from across the table. What a time it had been, but she was making things right. It was like a reset. She sipped her wine and turned to Hannah, Tom's mom.

"This is delicious, Hannah," she said.

"My pleasure, Dear," Hannah replied.

Tom squeezed Valerie's hand underneath the table.

The case was finished. Hal Borchardt was in custody and was going to undergo complete psychiatric evaluation. Valerie had no doubt he'd be put away for life, most probably in a maximum security psychiatric prison.

She felt sorry for him in a way. He wasn't completely responsible for his actions, but innocent people needed to be protected from killers, whether they were in control or not.

Though Valerie wished she could have saved all of Hal Borchardt's victims, she was pleased to know that his last intended victim, the woman he had taken to the amusement park, was going to make a full recovery.

This made her feel it was all worthwhile. That and stopping Hal from killing any number of other women

Charlie and Will had flown back to Quantico. They were all getting some downtime. Valerie smiled at the thought of Charlie getting to spend time with his kids.

Then she thought for a moment that she strangely didn't know much about Will's private life at all.

"You okay?" Tom said from beside her, the candles on the table glinting in his eyes.

"I am," Valerie said. "I am so sorry for running out on you all the last time I was here."

"That's all right," Tom's dad said. "I read about the killer you caught in the papers. That was some work."

"It was," she said.

"When I read about the type of work you do," Hannah continued Mark's words. "It made sense why you were so tense. It can't be easy dealing with those sorts of things.

"It isn't," Valerie said. "But I want to be truthful."

There was silence for a moment.

"The reason I freaked out the last time," Valerie explained. "Was because of my past. And I'd like to let you know what that was. I'm done hiding things from people anymore."

Tom squeezed Valerie's hand again in support.

She took a deep breath, looked at Tom's parents and said: "Let me tell you about my parents."

*

The orderly opened the door and gestured for Valerie to go in. Part of her didn't want to, but if those last few days had taught her anything, it was that mental health issues had to be dealt with head-on.

She didn't want to end up like her sister and mother, and so she had to confront her past to make a better future.

She was going to deal with her own issues until she had some answers from her mother.

Gwen sat on her bed, her hands tied as Valerie entered. She was scratching her left knee, Valerie could see that she had bled there.

"Mom," she said. "Please don't do that. Do you want me to get the nurse?"

Gwen pulled her patient robe down over the cuts, and looked up at the ceiling, wide-eyed.

Every time she saw her mom and the condition she was in, it was like a shot to her heart.

But today, there was one question on her mind. One that had to be answered.

"Mom," Valerie said softly. "What happened to my dad?"

Gwen stared at the ceiling and let out a horrid laugh.

"Which one?"

Valerie was confused.

"Your real dad or the one who pretended to be?" her mother turned and grinned at Valerie.

"Mom... What do you mean?"

"You think the man you remember was your father? Well he wasn't!" Gwen fell back onto her bed and then started breathing heavily. "Now leave me alone."

"Mom, please."

"Go do some detective work, big shot FBI Agent... See if you can find him... 17 Sycamore Avenue..." she said cackling. "Maybe you'll find him there... Now get out!"

Gwen screamed loudly over and over, and no matter what Valerie tried to do to calm her, she had to leave with her questions unanswered.

Valerie was stunned as she left the room.

Was it true? Did Valerie not know who her real dad was? Her mind was ablaze with terrible possibilities. Most of all, one question now burned into her mind: Who was the man she had called father, and what had happened to him?

All Valerie had to go on was the address her mom had given her: 17 Sycamore Avenue. It was time to go there and see how deep this rabbit hole truly was.

NOW AVAILABLE!

NO SLEEP
(A Valerie Law FBI Suspense Thriller—Book 4)

From #1 bestselling mystery and suspense author Blake Pierce comes book #4 in a gripping new series: a string of murders in subways and homeless encampments bears all the mark of a killer escaped from a local mental hospital. When the FBI's new unit targeting criminally-insane killers is assigned, Special Agent Valerie Law suspects this killer may not fit the profile—and may be more sinister than anyone expects.

"A masterpiece of thriller and mystery."
—Books and Movie Reviews, Roberto Mattos (re *Once Gone*)

NO SLEEP is book #4 in a new series by #1 bestselling mystery and suspense author Blake Pierce.

A page-turning crime thriller featuring a brilliant and haunted new female protagonist, the VALERIE LAW mystery series is packed with suspense and driven by a breakneck pace that will keep you turning pages late into the night. Fans of Rachel Caine, Teresa Driscoll and Robert Dugoni are sure to fall in love.

Books #5 and #6 in the series—NO QUARTER and NO CHANCE—are now also available.

"An edge of your seat thriller in a new series that keeps you turning pages! ...So many twists, turns and red herrings... I can't wait to see what happens next."
—Reader review (*Her Last Wish*)

"A strong, complex story about two FBI agents trying to stop a serial killer. If you want an author to capture your attention and have you guessing, yet trying to put the pieces together, Pierce is your author!"
—Reader review (*Her Last Wish*)

"A typical Blake Pierce twisting, turning, roller coaster ride suspense thriller. Will have you turning the pages to the last sentence of the last chapter!!!"
—Reader review (*City of Prey*)

"Right from the start we have an unusual protagonist that I haven't seen done in this genre before. The action is nonstop… A very atmospheric novel that will keep you turning pages well into the wee hours."
—Reader review (*City of Prey*)

"Everything that I look for in a book… a great plot, interesting characters, and grabs your interest right away. The book moves along at a breakneck pace and stays that way until the end. Now on go I to book two!"
—Reader review (*Girl, Alone*)

"Exciting, heart pounding, edge of your seat book… a must read for mystery and suspense readers!"
—Reader review (*Girl, Alone*)

Blake Pierce

Blake Pierce is the USA Today bestselling author of the RILEY PAGE mystery series, which includes seventeen books. Blake Pierce is also the author of the MACKENZIE WHITE mystery series, comprising fourteen books; of the AVERY BLACK mystery series, comprising six books; of the KERI LOCKE mystery series, comprising five books; of the MAKING OF RILEY PAIGE mystery series, comprising six books; of the KATE WISE mystery series, comprising seven books; of the CHLOE FINE psychological suspense mystery, comprising six books; of the JESSE HUNT psychological suspense thriller series, comprising twenty four books; of the AU PAIR psychological suspense thriller series, comprising three books; of the ZOE PRIME mystery series, comprising six books; of the ADELE SHARP mystery series, comprising fifteen books, of the EUROPEAN VOYAGE cozy mystery series, comprising four books; of the new LAURA FROST FBI suspense thriller, comprising nine books (and counting); of the new ELLA DARK FBI suspense thriller, comprising eleven books (and counting); of the A YEAR IN EUROPE cozy mystery series, comprising nine books, of the AVA GOLD mystery series, comprising six books (and counting); of the RACHEL GIFT mystery series, comprising eight books (and counting); of the VALERIE LAW mystery series, comprising nine books (and counting); of the PAIGE KING mystery series, comprising six books (and counting); of the MAY MOORE mystery series, comprising six books (and counting); and the CORA SHIELDS mystery series, comprising three books (and counting).

An avid reader and lifelong fan of the mystery and thriller genres, Blake loves to hear from you, so please feel free to visit www.blakepierceauthor.com to learn more and stay in touch.

BOOKS BY BLAKE PIERCE

CORA SHIELDS MYSTERY SERIES
UNDONE (Book #1)
UNWANTED (Book #2)
UNHINGED (Book #3)

MAY MOORE SUSPENSE THRILLER
NEVER RUN (Book #1)
NEVER TELL (Book #2)
NEVER LIVE (Book #3)
NEVER HIDE (Book #4)
NEVER FORGIVE (Book #5)
NEVER AGAIN (Book #6)

PAIGE KING MYSTERY SERIES
THE GIRL HE PINED (Book #1)
THE GIRL HE CHOSE (Book #2)
THE GIRL HE TOOK (Book #3)
THE GIRL HE WISHED (Book #4)
THE GIRL HE CROWNED (Book #5)
THE GIRL HE WATCHED (Book #6)

VALERIE LAW MYSTERY SERIES
NO MERCY (Book #1)
NO PITY (Book #2)
NO FEAR (Book #3)
NO SLEEP (Book #4)
NO QUARTER (Book #5)
NO CHANCE (Book #6)
NO REFUGE (Book #7)
NO GRACE (Book #8)
NO ESCAPE (Book #9)

RACHEL GIFT MYSTERY SERIES
HER LAST WISH (Book #1)
HER LAST CHANCE (Book #2)
HER LAST HOPE (Book #3)
HER LAST FEAR (Book #4)
HER LAST CHOICE (Book #5)
HER LAST BREATH (Book #6)
HER LAST MISTAKE (Book #7)
HER LAST DESIRE (Book #8)

AVA GOLD MYSTERY SERIES
CITY OF PREY (Book #1)
CITY OF FEAR (Book #2)
CITY OF BONES (Book #3)
CITY OF GHOSTS (Book #4)
CITY OF DEATH (Book #5)
CITY OF VICE (Book #6)

A YEAR IN EUROPE
A MURDER IN PARIS (Book #1)
DEATH IN FLORENCE (Book #2)
VENGEANCE IN VIENNA (Book #3)
A FATALITY IN SPAIN (Book #4)

ELLA DARK FBI SUSPENSE THRILLER
GIRL, ALONE (Book #1)
GIRL, TAKEN (Book #2)
GIRL, HUNTED (Book #3)
GIRL, SILENCED (Book #4)
GIRL, VANISHED (Book 5)
GIRL ERASED (Book #6)
GIRL, FORSAKEN (Book #7)
GIRL, TRAPPED (Book #8)
GIRL, EXPENDABLE (Book #9)
GIRL, ESCAPED (Book #10)
GIRL, HIS (Book #11)

LAURA FROST FBI SUSPENSE THRILLER

ALREADY GONE (Book #1)
ALREADY SEEN (Book #2)
ALREADY TRAPPED (Book #3)
ALREADY MISSING (Book #4)
ALREADY DEAD (Book #5)
ALREADY TAKEN (Book #6)
ALREADY CHOSEN (Book #7)
ALREADY LOST (Book #8)
ALREADY HIS (Book #9)

EUROPEAN VOYAGE COZY MYSTERY SERIES
MURDER (AND BAKLAVA) (Book #1)
DEATH (AND APPLE STRUDEL) (Book #2)
CRIME (AND LAGER) (Book #3)
MISFORTUNE (AND GOUDA) (Book #4)
CALAMITY (AND A DANISH) (Book #5)
MAYHEM (AND HERRING) (Book #6)

ADELE SHARP MYSTERY SERIES
LEFT TO DIE (Book #1)
LEFT TO RUN (Book #2)
LEFT TO HIDE (Book #3)
LEFT TO KILL (Book #4)
LEFT TO MURDER (Book #5)
LEFT TO ENVY (Book #6)
LEFT TO LAPSE (Book #7)
LEFT TO VANISH (Book #8)
LEFT TO HUNT (Book #9)
LEFT TO FEAR (Book #10)
LEFT TO PREY (Book #11)
LEFT TO LURE (Book #12)
LEFT TO CRAVE (Book #13)
LEFT TO LOATHE (Book #14)
LEFT TO HARM (Book #15)

THE AU PAIR SERIES
ALMOST GONE (Book#1)
ALMOST LOST (Book #2)
ALMOST DEAD (Book #3)

CUL DE SAC (Book #3)
SILENT NEIGHBOR (Book #4)
HOMECOMING (Book #5)
TINTED WINDOWS (Book #6)

KATE WISE MYSTERY SERIES
IF SHE KNEW (Book #1)
IF SHE SAW (Book #2)
IF SHE RAN (Book #3)
IF SHE HID (Book #4)
IF SHE FLED (Book #5)
IF SHE FEARED (Book #6)
IF SHE HEARD (Book #7)

THE MAKING OF RILEY PAIGE SERIES
WATCHING (Book #1)
WAITING (Book #2)
LURING (Book #3)
TAKING (Book #4)
STALKING (Book #5)
KILLING (Book #6)

RILEY PAIGE MYSTERY SERIES
ONCE GONE (Book #1)
ONCE TAKEN (Book #2)
ONCE CRAVED (Book #3)
ONCE LURED (Book #4)
ONCE HUNTED (Book #5)
ONCE PINED (Book #6)
ONCE FORSAKEN (Book #7)
ONCE COLD (Book #8)
ONCE STALKED (Book #9)
ONCE LOST (Book #10)
ONCE BURIED (Book #11)
ONCE BOUND (Book #12)
ONCE TRAPPED (Book #13)
ONCE DORMANT (Book #14)
ONCE SHUNNED (Book #15)
ONCE MISSED (Book #16)

ONCE CHOSEN (Book #17)

MACKENZIE WHITE MYSTERY SERIES
BEFORE HE KILLS (Book #1)
BEFORE HE SEES (Book #2)
BEFORE HE COVETS (Book #3)
BEFORE HE TAKES (Book #4)
BEFORE HE NEEDS (Book #5)
BEFORE HE FEELS (Book #6)
BEFORE HE SINS (Book #7)
BEFORE HE HUNTS (Book #8)
BEFORE HE PREYS (Book #9)
BEFORE HE LONGS (Book #10)
BEFORE HE LAPSES (Book #11)
BEFORE HE ENVIES (Book #12)
BEFORE HE STALKS (Book #13)
BEFORE HE HARMS (Book #14)

AVERY BLACK MYSTERY SERIES
CAUSE TO KILL (Book #1)
CAUSE TO RUN (Book #2)
CAUSE TO HIDE (Book #3)
CAUSE TO FEAR (Book #4)
CAUSE TO SAVE (Book #5)
CAUSE TO DREAD (Book #6)

KERI LOCKE MYSTERY SERIES
A TRACE OF DEATH (Book #1)
A TRACE OF MURDER (Book #2)
A TRACE OF VICE (Book #3)
A TRACE OF CRIME (Book #4)
A TRACE OF HOPE (Book #5)